Amy and Her Brothers
OR LOVE AND LABOR

BY
SARAH S. BAKER

1860

LAMPLIGHTER
Publishing
BUILDING CHRISTLIKE CHARACTER ... ONE STORY AT A TIME

Amy and Her Brothers.
Copyright © 2002 by Mark Hamby
All rights reserved.
First Printing, May, 2003
Second Printing, February 2005
Third Printing, March 2008
Fourth Printing, September 2010
Fifth Printing, September 2012
Sixth Printing, December 2014
Seventh Printing, February 2016
Eighth Printing, August 2016
Ninth Printing, December 2016
Tenth Printing, November 2018
Eleventh Printing, April 2020
Twelfth Printing, August 2020

Published by Lamplighter Publishing; a division of Lamplighter
Ministries International, Inc.

Printed at the Lamplighter Bindery, Mount Morris, NY.

The Lamplighter Collection is a family collection of rare books
from the 17th, 18th and 19th centuries. Each edition is printed in
an attractive hard-bound collector's format. For more information,
call us at 1-888-A-GOSPEL (1-888-246-7735) or 1-570-585-1314,
visit us at *www.lamplighter.net* or write:

> Lamplighter Publishing
> 23 State Street
> Mount Morris, NY

Author: Sarah S. Baker
Executive Editor: Mark Hamby
Chief Editor: Deborah Hamby
Historical Research: Darlene Catlett
Copy Editors: Darlene Catlett, Deborah Hamby
Layout and Design: Jana Phillips
Cover Design: Michal Rudolph

ISBN10: 1-58474-045-0
ISBN13: 978-1-58474-045-2
Adv9Maroon, K900, S23-RL

CONTENTS.

PREFACE.

As I write these remarks, I am sitting in a hospital waiting room. Loved ones wait to hear their names called over the intercom. Each family handles the stress of waiting with a mixture of fear, anxiety, soberness, laughter, and tears. I wait for news of my dad as he is having his fourth major surgery at this moment. Each surgery has been a test, but as the prophet Hosea proclaims:

> *"Come let us return unto the LORD; for He hath torn, and He will heal us; He hath smitten, and He will bind us up. After two days will He revive us; in the third day He will raise us up, and we shall live in His sight. Then shall we know, if we follow on to know the LORD."*

Approximately fifty families are waiting, but one in particular catches my attention. They have just received their phone call from the doctor who, apparently, no longer visits in person. The family includes a young man of about thirty, maybe younger. He is handsome, with dark hair and a charismatic smile. The doctor's words are not of comfort.

He hangs up the phone, faces his large family of about a dozen loved ones, and shares the news about his lovely wife. Her leg had to be removed. The family is stunned. No one speaks for a few moments. Then two get up simultaneously to comfort this brave young husband. Tears are shed by all.

Can anything be said that would bring comfort? Can good really come out of this? My thoughts are interrupted as I hear the husband's tender words, "I've been praying that God would help her to adjust if it came to this."

Yes, my friends, there is a God who can help in times of trouble. David of old said that "this poor man cried and the Lord heard, and delivered him from all his troubles." The road may not be easy, but we are assured that "the suffering of this present time is not worthy to be compared to the glory that shall he revealed in us."

In every world-worn man there is a human heart that craves a God to trust, a Christ to lean upon—an unsatisfied heart.

Amy and Her Brothers once again reminds me that God is good and that we can trust him no matter how difficult life's circumstances seem to be. As usual, I had to dry my eyes at the end of this story. Though we cannot always understand why, we can rest in the truth that God is forever faithful and loves us more than we can imagine. He works all things for our good and His glory. He is a God who feels our pain.

What I love most about this story is how the heartache and innocent faith of an orphan child paints a real-life picture of the hidden suffering all around me, challenging me to be more attentive to the hurts of those nearby.

It is my prayer that this precious story will open our hearts to the suffering that lurks all around us, within our communities and churches; and in so doing, will inspire us to plant seeds that will bring forth glorious fruit.

Because of His grace,
Mark Hamby
Philippians 2:4

Amy and Her Brothers

Or Love and Labor

CHAPTER I.

Amy's Home.

"I WONDER that old house was not pulled down long ago!" said Mr. Alden, as he looked at a queer little building he had passed a hundred times before.

There it stood, a narrow, two-story house, crowded in between its tall, stately neighbors, and looking very much out of place in the respectable street on which it fronted.

The moss was thick upon its roof; that was a sign of age, truly, and who could doubt that those windows with the small panes, and that door, divided in the middle, were made more than fifty years ago?

It was a stirring Monday morning, and Mr. Alden was on his way to his

place of business, yet he was in too
much of a hurry to see what was to
be seen, and to have his own thoughts
by the way. He was looking full at the
house in question, when the upper half
of the heavy door was opened, while a
voice from within said:

"Go now, like good boys, and come
back as soon as you can."

"I'll go, if Will carries the basket,"
said a lad about twelve years of age,
who now opened the lower half of the
door, and stood doubtfully on the sill.

"That I will," said a hearty, cheery
voice, and in another moment a smaller
boy appeared, with a great basket on
his arm.

The brown jug that lay in the basket
would have looked very suspicious to a
careless observer, but such was not Mr.
Alden. The besmeared bit of corn-cob
that served as a stopper, and a slight
stickiness on the sides of the jug, assured him that nothing more dangerous
than molasses had kept company with
it in times past.

Mr. Alden would have been fond
of flowers and shrubs, if he had lived
in the country; no doubt he would

have been quite a gardener in his own way. As it was, he could not go out in the fresh spring mornings, to dig up anemones from the woods, and plant them beside his pet hyacinths. He could not wade knee-deep in a marsh to get a bright cardinal flower, or plunge up to his neck in a pond to gather the sweet water-lilies.

Mr. Alden did not pine after the country now, though he had been a real lover of nature when a boy. He had found something, even in the crowded city, in which he could take a similar joy.

There was something fresh and natural and full of variety that Mr. Alden loved and cherished in his own home, and noted and watched in his daily walks.

Children, one, two and three, he could count at his own fireside, but that did not satisfy him, he must have a peep into every young face that crossed his path; he must catch every childish word that was uttered in his hearing.

You may be sure that the boys with the basket were quite as interesting to him as any new book that could have been opened before his eyes on a winter evening. "I say, Will, you take up all the road with your big basket; can't you give a fellow room?" said the elder of the two.

Will quietly changed the basket to his other arm, a proceeding which was quite welcome to him, to judge from the working of the freed shoulder, which seemed to rejoice to get rid of its burden.

It was plain that Will liked to carry the basket. He bent his little figure so as to half-sustain it with his hip, and moved cheerfully along, as he said: "I wish I was a man, I tell you what it is. I'd make a row, wouldn't I, Pick?"

"You'd be taken up, and then what would be the good of it?" said Pick contemptuously.

"Pooh! I don't mean that kind of a row. I mean I'd be somebody. I'd build a big house, and have a yellow satin sofa for Amy to lie on. I wouldn't have any bills; no, I wouldn't. I'd pay my cash down for what I wanted, and the rest I'd lay up in the bank. I tell you, when I'm a man, you'll see a hard-workin' fellow."

"You must be an industrious boy, if you want to be an industrious man," Mr. Alden opened his mouth to say, but he shut it suddenly. He would not remind the little lads that they had an observer close at their heels.

Pick put his hands in his pockets, and stepped on before Will, as if ashamed to be in his company, as they now turned into a more crowded street, and met several ladies and gentlemen.

"I say, Pick," continued Will, quite unconscious of the wish to drop him, "didn't you go to bed last night? You've got on your Sunday suit. What will Amy say to that?"

"She may say what she pleases. I an't going out with those old patched trowsers on again. You can see the pieces on the knees, a whole block off."

"An't our Amy a first-rate patcher, though? When she took up those trowsers, I didn't think she could make out; but they'd be as good as new, if they were all the same color; but I wouldn't mind that. Look at mine." and Will lifted his checked apron and showed the various shades of brown with which his little gray pants were repaired with wonderful neatness.

"Don't, Will, somebody'll see you," said Pick, strutting along in his Sunday suit. A neat little suit, it once had been good dark cloth, with jacket and trowsers to match; but now it was plain it had seen its best days, and Pick would have to stop growing at once, or wear black velvet ribbons round the bare wrists and ankles, that were becoming too conspicuous.

The boys now turned into a grocery-store, and Mr. Alden went his way, not, however, until he had looked into Will's round face and clear blue eyes, with a pleasant smile, and given Pick's small, self-satisfied countenance a less agreeable glance.

Quite a contrast to Mr. Alden's parting smile, was the reception that Will met at the grocer's hands. Was the man really so busy weighing out sugar and putting up crackers, that he did not see the boy?

Will supposed so, of course, and waited patiently for the tide of customers to roll by, and give him a chance. The river's ceaseless flow was nothing to it! Why, the man did not seem to have time even to turn his eyes to the spot where Will stood, leaning against the barrel on which he had perched his basket.

There was nothing to be done but to dash in boldly, and claim his share of attention. Will came to this conclusion when Pick had stood at least five minutes looking through the glass door; and Will had spelt out all the names on the neatly-painted boxes in which "Souchong," "Ind," "Tal-Can," and other mysterious articles of trade were stored.

"Please, sir," said Will, with a bow, "please, sir, I'd like this jug filled with molasses, and a peck of corn-meal put in this bag."

Will put the jug and bag side by side on the counter, but the shop-keeper seemed to wait for him to lay down something else, which did not appear to be forthcoming.

"The money, boy, where's the money?" said the grocer, with a stern look. "I can't trust your folks any more."

There was a sound of somebody shutting the glass door very quietly. Pick had disappeared.

"Why can't you trust us?" said Will,

with a flushed face. "We are honest, I'd say that before all the world."

"Honest folks pay their debts," said the grocer, turning away with a shrug.

"What do we owe you?" said Will, standing up as straight, and looking as independent as if he expected to discharge the whole debt at once.

"Sev-en-teen dol-lars!" said the man, dwelling upon every syllable, as if to make the amount more appalling. "I can't trust your folks any more."

Will took up his basket and silently left the store.

He did not feel like a man, as he stepped along the street. Tears, hot tears were running down his cheeks, and he did not care who saw them. He knew that a bill was a thing that Amy dreaded. He knew that she had a little bundle of greasy papers over which she often bent with an anxious look—bills he was sure they were—unpaid bills, but that any of them could ever have reached an alarming amount, he had not dreamed. That any one should think sister Amy was not honest, and refuse to trust her any more was a depth of misery his imagination had never pictured.

Will was but a child, just eleven years old, and, child-like, real tears were the first expression of his trouble.

Not a trace of them appeared, however, when he pushed open the heavy double-door, and stepped at once into the family sitting-room.

"Amy," he began, "I want to see you alone." But one look around the little circle made it plain that Pick had been the first bearer of the evil tidings.

Sister Amy's pale face was a little paler than usual, and it wore an anxious, troubled air, instead of its usual calm.

A dark-eyed little girl, two years younger than Will, was walking up and down the small room, exclaiming with an indignant stamp of the foot: "'Tis a shame! The hateful man! I say, it's a shame!" Pick looked perfectly crestfallen, and was biting his nails most industriously.

"Come, children, we must take our breakfast now, or you will all be late for school," said Amy, trying to speak cheerfully. "I meant to have some cakes and molasses for you this morning, but here is plenty of bread, enough for us all. Go, Harry, and get that nice cold sausage-fat you put in the cupboard yesterday. That will be better than butter."

Little Harriet's face brightened, and she soon placed the small earthen dish beside the loaf, on the table. No tea nor coffee, milk nor sugar appeared at that breakfast, but the water was cold and clear, and the children were hungry. Slice after slice were consumed by Harry and Pick. Amy, too, managed to eat a great many mouthfuls; but there was something rising and swelling in Will's throat, that seemed to take the place of breakfast for him.

"Now, off with you to school. Come, Harriet, let me brush your hair," said Amy pleasantly, as soon as the meal was over.

"I am not going to school this morning," said Will decidedly. Pick and Harriet looked at him in wonder, and Amy cast upon him a reproachful glance, as she spoke the gentle reproof, "*My* Willy!"

"Please, sister," said Willy, and Amy's displeasure changed to tenderness, as she saw the unwonted tears gathering in the eyes of her merry-hearted brother.

Pick and Harriet seemed to have forgotten all about grocers and grocers' bills. Away they went to the school, as cheerful and tidy as if there were no such thing as want in the world.

CHAPTER II.

A Partner in Business.

WILL had always been fond of lending a helping hand to "Sister Amy." He could not bear to see her going about with her slow, limping motion, when his steps would do as well. He knew very certainly that her busy mornings were to be paid for by afternoons of pain, weary afternoons on the old couch by the wall. He had seen her there too often, trying to sew, when she could not sit up, and smiling as if there were a great deal of fun in the experiment.

Will always liked to help his sister, but on this particular morning he seemed possessed with the spirit of activity. Boy's work or girl's work, it was all the same to him. Washing dishes, sweeping pavement, chopping wood, dusting and cleaning up generally, seemed quite in his line.

At last all was tidy in the little home, and Amy sat down on the old couch. She did not press her hand to her side, or speak of the pain in her back. "Come, Willy, now tell me what you have been thinking about," she said, and she put out her thin hand towards her brother.

Willy took his seat close at her side, and her arm went round him. He dropped his head on her knee and for a moment was silent.

"Don't be troubled, Willy dear," she said. "Nothing new has happened."

"Yes, but I did not know. I did not understand about it before. You kept it all to yourself, Amy, and that is what has made you look so worried over your papers."

"The Lord will take care of us. He never forsakes the orphan," said Amy quietly.

"How much do we owe?" asked Will, with a business-like air.

Amy looked earnestly at her brother for a moment and then said, "Give me the old atlas from the corner cupboard."

Amy was not going to teach a geography lesson. She had bent over that atlas a great deal of late, but Europe and Australia, Asia and California had been all unnoticed by her anxious eyes. Again and again she had studied the figures that were between the maps, again and again she had added up their sum total on the back of a letter; she did not need to go over it now. Yet with Will looking over her shoulder, she read aloud the items of each bill, and at last summed them up once more, Will repeating each addition to himself as she went on.

"Twenty-five dollars in all, you see, Will. That is not such a terrible sum," she said, trying to smile, but tears came in her eyes.

Will had been on the verge of weeping too, an instant before, but all such feelings vanished in a moment.

He felt changed, as it were, suddenly into a man, a helpful, active, tender-hearted man. Why, it was his business to comfort his sister, to keep up her courage, and to take care of her! What had he to do with tears!

"Twenty-five dollars!" (He named

the sum quite boldly now.) "Twenty-five dollars! Why, that's but a trifle, Amy. I read of a man in the paper the other day who owed two hundred thousand dollars, and could not pay a cent of it, and he had been a rich man too. That was a debt worth talking about. We must manage this. I don't doubt it can be done. So don't you be down-hearted, Amy. It's the boy's business to see to matters of the house. I'm sure I might do that, when I've such a dear good sister to keep things straight at home. Now, Amy, we won't talk any more about it to-day, but I'll just have it in mind, and may be by to-morrow, we may begin to see things mend."

Amy looked into the boy's young cheerful face and drew him tenderly to her side. She kissed him in silence. She knew he was but a child; she looked for no real aid from him, but she could not help taking courage from his bold, hopeful words. It was a comfort at least to talk over with someone the anxieties that had been weighing upon her.

Poor Amy! She had not been willing to cast a shadow over Will's young life: but now that he knew so much, and felt so deeply, it could do him no harm to know how matters really stood. She had told him all, and yet he did not seem crushed, but stood up beside her looking more bright, manly, and loving than ever before.

Very dear was her brother to her then, very welcome was his sympathy, but she did not forget the Friend who "sticketh closer than a brother," and who had been her comforter when no human friend knew her cares.

"Will," she said earnestly, "God can bring us safely out of all our difficulties. When I think of that, nothing troubles me."

"Yes, Amy, I've been thinking that in my heart, though I did not like to say it out. I feel just as sure He'll put it right for us, as if we had the money in the bank."

Will spoke truly. He knew that God was his Friend; he knew the precious promises to the fatherless and the stranger; and the sudden manliness that had come over him was strengthened and staid by the thought of the omnipotent arm on which he had a right to lean.

CHAPTER III.

A Glimpse at the Past.

AMY HOWE was only seventeen. She had never known health, but she had the better blessings of a calm, peaceful spirit, and a loving heart. Amy had lived for others, ever since little Harriet was left a motherless babe, with two lisping brothers smiling beside her cradle, when all about them were weeping.

To watch over the little ones, to keep them neat and tidy, and to make home bright for them, had been Amy's office. Her father had lost heart after the death of his wife, and never rallied. He was little at his own fireside, and too much where false merriment tries to take the place of calm cheerfulness, and evil companions tempt and lead astray.

At one time he was a book-keeper, then an editor, then he tried daguerreotyping, and at last made a poor subsistence by copying law-papers.

An aged relative left him, by will, the old-fashioned house which his children now occupied. He was used to a roving life. It cost him no effort to leave his home in Ohio, and move to an eastern city, that he might once more have a roof to call his own.

The expense of the journey had gone far to empty his purse, when sudden sickness laid him low. In a few short days after the old double-door had first opened to him, he was carried forth from it to his last resting-place; and his children were left orphans. Amy comforted the little ones, sent them to school, tasked her own strength to make their home neat and cheerful, and spent sparingly from the little still left of her father's earnings. The accounts which Mr. Howe's respectable appearance had enabled him to commence, Amy had kept up, while through the sleepless nights and busy days she tried to plan for the future. Plan, we say, if that can be called planning, which was anxious wishing for relief, ending in a feeling of utter helplessness, and a casting of care on Him who loves to give the weary rest.

When Amy laid her head on her pillow, the night after her conference with Willy, she felt as though she had lost one half of her burden. Willy's hopefulness, and her own faith, seemed to come hand in hand to comfort her, and she fell into a sweet sleep, such sweet sleep as it is the right of every Christian to enjoy.

Let those who have no Heavenly Friend spend their nights in weary dwelling on care and sorrow, but "*He* giveth his beloved sleep." Those who trust in the Lord need fear no evil.

CHAPTER IV.

The Travelling Advertisement.

WILLY HOWE'S school-days were over. On that he was determined. Not that he disliked study; if he had been a drone or a dunce he could never have stood first in his class, when column after column of hard words and harder definitions were recited from the dictionary; he could not have drawn off-hand a map of Europe, which the master said he could not better himself. No, no, Willy wrote a clear, round hand; he could not be puzzled in Lovell's Arithmetic; he was a good speller, and moreover, could have found his way in a pretty extensive tour through the civilized world, without a guide-book.

Willy loved study, and thanks to the excellent schooling he received, he had obtained an education, which was to him a priceless treasure. Now, he rightly concluded that he was not called upon to pore over his books, while on his dear, delicate sister fell all the burden of the family.

When Willy awoke the morning after his day at home with Amy, his first feeling was an unusual sense of care. This was to him but as the noise of the far-off battle to the soldier which makes him seize his armor, and make ready for the conflict.

Willy had no coward heart. His memory at once brought up to him the hard fighting that was before him, and he hastened to seek the strength which would be sure to bring him off victorious.

Before Pick had opened his sleepy eyes, Willy was up and dressed. From his Bible he had read words that made him feel ready for anything that was before him; on his knees he had asked God to bless all his undertakings, and help him to be to his sister a true friend in time of need.

What wonder that Willy's face was bright and joyous, when Pick, with a yawn, asked peevishly if it was time to get up.

"See for yourself, Pick," said Willy, throwing open the shutters, and letting the sunlight stream in. "See for yourself, and come to your own conclusion, while I go down to sweep the pavement."

"The top of the morning to you, Amy," said Will, as he peeped into the kitchen, on the way to the street.

Amy's good-morning was less buoyant, but her smile was very sweet, and Will felt as he went to his work, that she was a sister worth doing anything for.

Harriet caught a glimpse of her brother's bright face, and bounded after him, to give him a full share of her conversation, while he was sweeping.

"See now," said Will, going to work most vigorously, "see if I don't get this pavement swept off before you count a hundred."

Harriet's little tongue rattled over the numbers as if it were crazy, and her merry laugh soon told Will that he was not quite such a fast sweeper as he had supposed.

Will's work was soon done, however, and both the children were going in, when their attention was attracted by a man coming up the street, carrying in his hand a paper-banner, which he seemed anxious that everybody should see. Will had a fancy for spelling out signs and placards, and he waited to read what was on the great banner.

"A menagerie, I guess," said Harriet, clapping her hands. "I mean to go."

The banner was by this time very near them, and Will had no thought to give his little sister's suppositions.

"TWENTY THOUSAND DOLLARS TO LEND!" was the interesting announcement that flared in great black letters from the white cambric of the travelling advertisement.

It did not take Will long to read every word, large print, small print, and all.

"Twenty thousand dollars to lend, on good security, watches, jewelry, and gold and silver generally, taken in pawn, and faithfully restored, when money and interest are paid."

Willy had his pencil out in a moment. The name of this mighty money-lender,

and the number of his office, were noted
down with the greatest care.

This business-like result of his ob-
servations being through, Harriet was
favored with two or three flying hops
from the upper door-step, and then was
carried off bodily into the sitting-room,
in spite of a laughing resistance on her
part.

After Pick and Harriet had finished
their simple breakfast, a conference
took place between Amy and Will. The
result of this conference was a secret
mission on the part of Will, which
he considered as honorable and mo-
mentous as an embassy to any of the
crowned heads of Europe.

In a most unattractive part of one of
the lower streets of the city, there was
a little dark shop, above the door of
which was the very name that Will had
noted down so carefully. To this shop
Will made his way, only stopping now
and then to press his hand to his side
and to see that his coat was buttoned
up tight.

Will had to look twice at his memo-
randum, to be sure that there was
no mistake about the name and the

number. It did not seem to him possible that such a grand, clear-looking advertisement could have come from such a dark, unattractive-looking spot, yet so it must be. There in the window, was a worn and faded sign: "Money to lend." There could be no mistake.

Will stepped in with rather an important look on his face, and before speaking he proceeded to unbutton his coat, and draw forth a plain gold watch, and to lay it on the counter.

"What is such a watch as that worth?" said Will, with his eyes fixed on the man behind the counter.

The pawnbroker pushed up his spectacles, stared first at the boy, then at the watch. Willy did not look like a thief, and the man knew it, yet he said suspiciously, "Did you steal it, eh, boy?"

Willy's face flushed as he answered, "It was my father's watch. He wore it twenty years. You'll find his name there in the inside. George Howe, that was my father's name."

Willy felt his throat choking up; he was actually afraid he should cry; and what a piece of business that would be for a boy, who expected to be the man of the family, and stand by his sister in his troubles.

"May be your father hain't gone so far as you make out. Boys have pawned old gentlemen's watches before for their own reasons," said the shop-keeper with another searching look.

Will was inclined to snatch up the watch indignantly, and leave the shop. The image of the grocer saying, "We can't trust your folks anymore," rose up before him, and he staid. He was silent for a moment. He had no friend in the city to whom he could appeal. At length he said desperately, "Come home with me if you please, and see my sister Amy. You can't think hard of her. We want to borrow twenty-five dollars, and you may as well know all about us."

The man looked at the watch, far exceeding in value the sum named, and then at the boy. There was truth in that young face, but the old pawnbroker had seen too much of the world to dare to trust even such a countenance.

"I've got to go up-town," he said, reaching down a dusty old hat, and a crooked walking-stick. "So you may take me to see this sister Amy."

Again there was a suspicious glance at the boy, to see how he took the acceptance of his proposition.

"If you see Amy, all will be right," said Willy, who had a wonderful confidence in his sister's power of pleasing.

They were a queer couple, the bent old man, and the young bright boy, yet no one noticed them, as they passed along the crowded streets. No one noticed them, we said, yet they were not unobserved by the great Ruler of events who had brought them together for His own wise purposes.

CHAPTER V.

The Old Visitor.

*L*ITTLE as Pickard Howe liked to get up in the morning, he was not fond of being late at school. After lounging away the time when he should have been making his preparations, he generally went off at last in a terrible flurry, leaving confusion and disorder behind him.

Amy had gathered up the scattered books that Pick had thrown down in his hurried search for his geography; she had put his "morning shoes" into the closet, and restored to its place the brush with which he had given the parting touches to his curly hair. The traces of Harriet's careless, reckless habits were even more in number, yet Amy had gone about patiently restoring order, without one unpleasant expression ruffling her countenance, or one unkind thought marring the peace in her heart.

The four rooms which the old-fashioned house contained had been severally visited and made neat and tidy by her skillful hands. Weary in body, she lay down on the old couch, but not to spend even a few short minutes in idleness.

The bland air of Indian summer was changing into the real keenness of autumn, and Amy well knew the little ones were but ill-prepared for winter. An old cloth cloak of her father she thought would be quite an inexhaustible mine of material for clothing the boys, and as she lay, her busy hands were ripping away the worn collar, while from time to time her eye measured the ample folds of the precious garment.

She heard the outer-door open. It must be Willy returning from his mission. What news had he to tell? Her eager, questioning face turned towards him, but she felt too weary to follow her natural inclination to rise and meet him.

She had not a moment for thought, when Willy and his companion entered.

"This is my sister, Amy, Mr. Dimer," said the boy. There was respect and affection in the tone; it was plain that sister Amy was in Willy's eyes one worth seeing.

"A lazy Miss! Lying down to work," thought the old man; but his face changed suddenly as Amy rose, and with an evident effort moved across the room, to hand the stranger a chair.

"You want to raise money on your father's watch," he began abruptly. "How am I to know George Howe was your father?"

The family Bible lay on the table. What a treasure it had proved to Amy in her loneliness and anxiety! Now it was to serve a new purpose.

Again Amy crossed the room, and the old man's face softened as he noted the misfortune that had marred her person, but traced no mark of repining on her sweet face. Amy threw open the Bible at the family record.

"You will read the history of our little family there," she said quietly.

Mr. Dimer put on his spectacles

and took the Bible on his knee. It was long since the Holy Book had lain open before him, that old dealer in money!

There was a truth in that simple record that could not be doubted. Born, married, died; so short, so full of meaning, so complete was the biographical sketch of the parents, while the birth alone of the orphan children was registered; those children who were now to struggle along life's pathway side by side.

There was something in that family history which seemed to touch the heart of the old man. It spoke to him of the shortness of human life; it whispered to him of pity for the orphan.

"Amy, that's you," he said reading, then looking full into the young girl's face.

"That is my name," said Amy quietly.

"Pickard! Nonsense; what a name! Is that you?" he continued, turning to Willy.

"I am William, mentioned below," said the boy, pointing out with his finger the date of his birth.

"You are not big of your age," said the old man disapprovingly.

"No; but I mean to do great things," said Will with a smile.

"Let me see the watch," said the old man thoughtfully.

Willy drew out the treasure again, and placed in Mr. Dimer's hands.

"Didn't your father leave you any money?" said the old man quickly.

"A little; but that is all gone, and we have debts beside, which we want to pay with the loan," said Willy, speaking up as the man of family.

"An't you uneasy? What do you expect to live on?" said the man, turning towards Amy. "You couldn't do much in the way of hard work."

"We own the house. It was left to my father by an old aunt. So the children will have a home. For the rest, I am sure the Lord will provide," said Amy simply.

The pawnbroker looked through his spectacles into Amy's sweet, placid face. The poor young stranger before him had security of which he knew nothing. His precious gains might be taken from him by fire, flood, dishonesty, or commercial charges, but Amy's portion was sure. She had an unfailing refuge in those few words: "The Lord will provide."

Mr. Dimer looked down. He had accidentally turned with his elbow the page that contained the family record, and now the last of Malachi lay open before him. His eye caught the words:

"For behold the day cometh, that shall burn as an oven; and all the proud, yea, and all that do wickedly, shall be stubble, and the day that cometh shall burn them up, saith the Lord of hosts, that it shall leave them neither root nor branch."

Like a swift arrow those words of denunciation seemed to pierce the heart of the old man; but turning from them he cast his eye up the page and read:

"And they shall be mine, saith the Lord of hosts, in that day when I make up my jewels."

He shut the book suddenly. Had he not read of the two portions in store for himself and the helpless strangers before him? He would not think of it, he would attend to the matter in hand. "How much—how much"—he said hesitatingly—"how much did you want to owe on the watch?"

"Twenty-five dollars," said Will, again acting spokesman.

Mr. Dimer took out a worn but well-filled pocket-book. Five five-dollar notes he laid on table.

Willy's eyes glistened, and he said joyously to his sister, "I knew the Lord would take care of us. Keep up heart, Amy."

"I am very, very much obliged to you, sir," Amy said warmly.

"I don't do you any great favor," said the man. "You will have to pay me half-yearly for use of the money, and I have the watch for security. You can have it back you know, when you return the money."

"May that be before a great while," said Willy cheerily.

Mr. Dimer rose to go. Childless and alone he lived, gathering up this world's goods, but enjoying them. There was a charm to him in those young trusting hearts and there was a message of power to him from that old family Bible.

Love on earth and a home in heaven seemed better to him then, than all the gold in Ophir.

The old man was gone; there was no excuse for his lingering there.

"O brother! I am so glad," said Amy, as she took the bank-notes in her hand. The other arm she passed round Willy, and side by side they knelt. That was real thanksgiving, not a mere saying of heartless, unmeaning words.

The God of the orphan was praised for all His mercies. The old stranger had a blessing called down on his unworthy head.

In every world-worn man there is a human heart that craves a God to trust, a Christ to lean upon—an unsatisfied heart.

This is hard to realize, and Amy would not have thought of seeking to give her faith to the man of loans and compound interest. Her calm trust had been better for him than a lengthy sermon.

CHAPTER VI.

The Grocer.

TRULY Amy and Will were young in the ways of the world. They had borrowed just enough to pay their debts, but what they were to live on afterwards, they did not know. Twenty-five dollars was the sum so fixed in their minds, that they had not thought it possible they could borrow more.

Undisturbed by any such anxieties, Will set off for the grocer's, feeling much like the man he had wanted to be only the day before, when he had carried the basket.

He had but to mention that he wished to pay his bill, and the grocer found time to attend to him in a moment. As the receipt was signed, Will said apologetically, "We should have been glad to pay you before, but we are orphans, and just beginning to take care of ourselves."

There was no appeal for sympathy in Will's cheerful manner, as he stated this simple fact; yet one word in his sentence had reached the hearer's heart.

The grocer had his own happy, rosy little ones nursed and guarded; could he hear the name of orphan without a pang?

God has promised to bless the fatherless, and one way in which He does it is, by turning all hearts tenderly towards them. Those who give to no other good cause, will open their purse for the orphan; those who never weep for their own sins, will shed a tear for the motherless, the fatherless, and the little ones left alone in the world.

The grocer made no direct reply to Willy's remark, but as he handed him the receipt he said, "Let me send your folks some uncommon wheat flour that has just come in, and some extra cheese, not to be put down in the bill, mind you, but just for them to taste."

"Thank you, sir," said Will, "sister Amy will be much obliged to you."

It was a satisfaction to the grocer to put up the generous parcels which he prepared for Willy, and as he did so, he murmured in his heart, "I did not mean to be hard upon orphans."

"What are we to do now, all our debts are paid?" said Amy as Will returned from the grocer's. She was really beginning to lean upon her young brother—so natural is it for a woman to look for some supporting arm.

"Why, I'm going to be a—a—I don't know exactly what line of business I shall go into, but I mean to be a regular driver," said Will cheerily. "But look here, see what Mr. Dobbs sent us, just to try his goods—sort of a present, you see. He was in such a good humor this morning."

Bread from the hand of the Lord it seemed to Amy.

"Give us this day our daily bread;" so our Lord teaches us to pray; who that is so provided need be anxious about the morrow?

CHAPTER VII.

Snow.

*A*MY was not glad to see the snow falling next morning; there were warm garments yet be finished; there was more wood to be bought, before she could rejoice at the coming of cold weather.

With a shout, Will received the news that the snow was half a foot deep. He sprang up with a merry twinkle in his eye. There was no doubt in his mind as to the line of business he should follow, for that morning at least.

The bit of pavement before the old house, he cleared off in the most satisfactory manner while Pick looked on from the window, Harriet pelted him with snow-balls while he worked.

"Now I am in for money-making,"

said Will, shouldering his shovel and giving a sweeping bow, as he prepared to set off. Pick threw up the window in a moment, and exclaimed, "You are not going, Will Howe, to clear off snow for other people!"

"That I will, gladly. I'm a worker," said Will, his shovel a flourish in the air as he departed.

Pick shut the window disdainfully, wondering how people could be so low in their tastes. Pick knew that their family fare had been growing plainer and plainer; he knew that the grocer had refused further credit, and that Amy had hard work to provide the comfortable clothing that would be needed for the winter, which seemed to have dropped suddenly upon them.

Pick knew this, but he asked for no particulars. He drove such disagreeable thoughts from his mind as things that did not concern him. The school cost nothing, and there he could go and prepare himself for the career which he fancied would in the end benefit him. Will might lower himself, if he pleased, with servile occupations, but he would follow his higher destiny.

Will did not think whether he was lowering himself or not. He was full of the merry, light-hearted spirit of boyhood, and there was fun to all that he undertook. He knew that the purse was empty, and yet he was not over-anxious as to his success in this, his first effort at earning his own living. Honest industry he felt to be the duty of the present—cheerful, honest industry— without a foreboding thought for that future, for which the Lord would surely provide.

It was an amusement to Will to mount the tall flights of steps, and inquire in his most pleasant manner whether he should clear off the snow. He liked to get a peep into the spacious halls. The very servants who opened the doors pleased him with their various styles of refusing or accepting his offers.

Will was fond of exercise; he actually liked work for its own sake. He found it no hardship to throw off the light snow, and when the bright silver was dropped into his hand for payment, it seemed to him to be almost rained down from some cloud with a silver lining that was passing overhead.

The pavements were all cleared, when a sudden thronging of the street with young faces reminded him that the schools were out, and he must be at home to take his dinner with the rest.

Turning a corner, he came suddenly upon Pick and Harriet. The little sister gave a bound towards him, and seized his free hand. Pick seemed well pleased to meet him too, for Pick had his own news to tell.

"We boys have got a new wrinkle," he began. "We are going to have a society made up of choice fellows—the tip-top of the school. We are going to write pieces and speak 'em; and someday the master says he'll let us have the school-room for an exhibition—won't that be fun?"

"No doubt it will," said the younger brother a little soberly. Amy's sweet pale face rose up before him, and the momentary regret for the step he had taken passed away. He had left school and its pleasures; but he had done right, there could be no doubt of that.

"I shall attend the exhibition, and sit on the front-seats with friends of the speakers," said Will in his usual merry way.

"Not with your snow-shovel in your hand, I hope, " said Pick.

"Speak well of the bridge that carries you over," said Will, taking from his pocket a handful of small change. "Seventy-five cents—all my own! What do you think of that, Pick?"

Pick's eyes brightened, and he said: "Now you ought to give a treat. You'll be real mean if you don't. See here, 'Hot oysters.' This is a first rate cellar, the fellows say. Come, let's go down." Pick put his foot on the first of the descending steps, but Will did not offer to follow him.

"No, I thank you, sir," said Will decidedly, as he dropped his change into his pocket with a tinkling sound, "sister Amy's my banker. What I get goes straight to her."

"Well, you are a mean fellow—a low, mean fellow," said Pick, strutting on as if quite ashamed to be in such company.

Will knew well enough who was the "mean fellow" then, and he was going to say so, but a whisper at his heart made him still.

Will felt that the last few days had

drawn him wonderfully near to his Heavenly Father. How could he break the law of love, the chief law of the God in whom he trusted? Pick might say what he pleased, Will was resolved to deal no harsh answers. There could be no quarrelling certainly, so long as all the fault was on one side.

Pick saw determination in Will's air, and with a careless whistle he walked on, leaving his brother and sister to follow.

"How stuck up Pick is! He ought to be ashamed!" said little Harriet, who was apt to be indignant on every possible occasion.

"Pick is a very smart boy," said Will; "I shouldn't wonder if he should turn out to be the best speaker in the school."

"That's just what he said himself, just before we met you," said Harriet naively.

"That is what everybody would say," Will said, laughing in spite of himself. "Pick only goes with the multitude. An't it queer, Harriet, I feel as if I was really grown up since I have left school."

"You haven't grown any, that I see,"

said Harriet, with a wondering look at
her brother.

"We all grow every day of our lives;
even men and women are growing," said
a pleasant voice behind the children.

Will remembered Mr. Alden's face
immediately. He did not often get such
an approving smile as that which had
greeted him in front of the grocer's
door.

Will touched his cap, and said,
"How's that, sir?" while Harriet opened
her eyes wide, and wondered what the
stranger meant by speaking to them.

Will had carried his shovel in mili-
tary style, over his shoulder, but now
he let it trail behind him as he listened
to Mr. Alden's reply.

"I don't mean that men and women
keep growing in their bodies. That
would be very inconvenient, and cost
us too many new suits of clothes. What
I mean is that everybody is growing
worse or better; and we may get on
very fast in both ways, in even a very
few days."

"I know it—I know it, sir," said Will
warmly.

"Then be sure to grow in the right

way, and always be good to sister Amy."
Here Mr. Alden said a hasty good-by,
and turning a corner, disappeared.

"How did he know anything about
sister Amy? Isn't he a queer man?" said
Harriet in surprise.

"I like him though," said Will.
"I mean to be a gentleman like him
when I grow up—a real kind-spoken
gentleman."

CHAPTER VIII.

Pick.

WILL'S patient industry knew no flagging. He was ready to do anything and everything that Providence threw in his way. One day he went on errands for the neighboring grocer; the next he carried carpet-bags for ladies at a deposit, in an opposite direction; and every snow-storm brought him in a sure harvest, the seed of which seemed to him sown directly by heaven.

Will had the pleasure of thinking that he was the man of the family—the out-of-door provider for in-door wants. He little knew that there was another source of revenue for their humble home than his uncertain earnings. He had not seen Amy working at her embroidery when the children were all away; he did not know that she was toiling when he was sleeping; he did not suspect how well "the lame girl" was becoming known at a certain fancy-store, and how many yards of embroidered trimming she sold there from time to time.

Amy would not sadden her young brother by the knowledge of her weary labor. His cheerfulness was very precious to her; he was doing all in his power; he should not know that for bare necessities she too must strain every nerve.

"Give Pick the best clothes—make Harriet look respectable," were Will's words. "I don't mind the patches; they suit my way of life."

So Pick kept on at school—at times a brilliant scholar, at times too lazy to learn even the simplest lessons. Pick hated what he called drudgery. He had an idea that he was to go through the world, and make a great figure without it.

There is drudgery, real elementary work, uninteresting work in every science, trade, profession. We must not despise the low rounds of the ladder, if we would mount to top. The multiplication-table must be learned if you would make a good Arithmetician. The Latin Grammar must be at your tongue's end, if you ever expect to read Caesar and Virgil. You must learn to mix colors, if you are to paint in oil. You must go over much dry chemistry before you can make a good doctor or apothecary. Work is everywhere, and in every calling. Those only escape it who are mere useless beings, mere cumberers of the earth.

The school debating society was much in Pick's thoughts, and now and then he might be seen at home in the evening, with a pencil in hand and a sheet of paper before him, on which he put down very grand and moral sentences on this duty or that virtue. Pick could be good on paper as well as anybody else, but he had not yet even begun to struggle against the selfishness that is the great sin of every human heart.

Pick's use of the pencil became more and more and frequent, as the winter went on, and at last he concluded to unite the exercises of the debating society with his usual quarterly public examination. Pickard Howe was to be one of speakers.

He had been reading his "piece" one evening in the little family circle, as a particular favor, he said, as perhaps they would not have a chance to hear him speak it. Will and Amy exchanged glances, and then listened in silence.

"That's first-rate," said Will, clapping his hands as Pick read the finishing sentence in his effective manner.

"You have done wonderfully well, Pick," said Amy quietly. A short pause followed, in which Amy was wondering whether Pick would ever follow out in practice the high principles about which he could so easily write.

Her meditations were disturbed by Pick's saying, in a fretful tone, "You are always patching Will's clothes, Amy. I should think you might find time to make me a little respectable for the examination."

Will's cheek flushed, but the angry words that sprang to his lips were checked by Amy's prompt but gentle answer.

"I'll do what I can for you, Pick. I wish I could get you a new coat."

"You might make me one out of that

best coat of father's, if you only chose,"
was Pick's reply.

"I hoped to keep that until you were
larger. It seems a pity to cut it up now,"
said Amy thoughtfully.

"Oh! yes; I suppose it is to be kept
for Master Willy. It's no matter what I
wear. I think the oldest ought to have
some rights at least."

Will jumped from the table, and ran
out into the cool night air. He dare not
trust himself in temptation one moment
longer, lest he should say something he
should repent.

Harriet had no idea of any such
government. Her indignation burst
forth at once, "You shan't speak so to
sister Amy, you great bad, lazy boy! I
wouldn't ever do another thing for you,
if I were in her place; no, I wouldn't."

"But I would," said Amy gently.
"Hush, Harriet! Pick, I'll try to make
over the coat for you. It is natural you
should want to be in order at such a
time."

"Of course it is. I wonder you didn't
think of that before," said Pick.

Amy knew there was no time to be
lost. She put the few last stitches into

the patch that she had been sewing into Will's only jacket, and then she set to work immediately to rip the coat in question.

When Will returned to the kitchen, the only warm room in the house, he found Pick reading away in a paper-covered book he had borrowed, while Amy was bending over the coat, with no lingering resentment in her sweet face. Her example had its natural effect. Will had his knife out in a moment. "Let me help you, Amy," he said. "Two hands can work faster than one."

"Don't cut the edges, Will," said Amy, pointing out to Will where he was to begin. A pleasant, affectionate smile passed between them, and they seemed very dear to each other then.

What so increases love among brethren as walking, hand in hand, in the heavenly path!

CHAPTER IX.

The Examination.

EXAMINATION DAY had come, and Pick was no laggard in bed that morning. Before the sun was fairly up, he was now pacing the kitchen, now declaiming, and now stopping to adjust his curling locks into the proper curve about his fair forehead.

"I hope you will pass a good examination," said Amy, as Pick was starting for school.

"That's a small matter if I do well with my piece," said Pick, as he disappeared.

Pick had not said one word to Will about being present at the examination; but Amy had spoken of it as a matter of course, from the first. She thought the industrious boy really deserved the relaxation and the pleasure the examination would afford.

"You will surprise Pick," she said cheerfully. "He does not think of your caring to go; so now make yourself tidy, and be off in time to get a good seat."

Pure water, brush and comb, clean collar and patched coat, helped to fit out Will for the important occasion. A dear, noble-looking boy he seemed to Amy, as she kissed him good-by, and bade him notice everything, in order to tell her all about the examination. Will went in at the door open for spectators, and found his way to a front seat.

"Keep your place, my lad," said a pleasant voice to him, soon after, when he rose to make room for some gentlemen.

Will knew the voice and the kind face, and he felt as though a friend were near him, when Mr. Alden sat down beside him.

Pickard Howe was the first speaker. A pretty boy anybody would have called him, as he came forward on the stage and made a very handsome bow.

His speech was really well written, and well delivered, and there was a murmur of approbation throughout the house as he closed. "Uncommonly well done," said Mr. Alden, addressing himself to Willy, who was clapping heartily, and looking at Pick with affectionate pride. "Uncommonly well done; don't you say so?"

"He's my brother," said Will with sparkling eyes, raising himself on the bench at the same time, that Pick might see him sharing his triumph.

It was plain that Pick did see him; but he turned quickly from the brother in the worn, patched coat, and walked off from the stage in another direction. Pick complained of being overcome by the effort he had made in speaking, and was excused, to go out and breathe the fresh air.

The boys were heard to say, "Pick Howe is sneaking the recitations," and there was truth in the rough remark. Pick knew very well he should lose his laurels when he stood up to recite.

With the promptness of a file of soldiers obeying their commanding officers on parade, class after class went through with its performances. The question was hardly dropped, when the answer was fired off by a score of voices. There had been drilling there beyond doubt.

Some of the visitors seemed anxious to know whether there was any real intelligence, any actual comprehension of the subjects touched upon, among the pupils.

The master encouraged free questioning, and the boys did wonderfully well, though the visitors tried hard to puzzle them.

At length a sum was given out, coming under one of the rules that had been so glibly recited. It was a difficult sum truly, and none of the boys dared to come up to the blackboard to work it out. The master looked annoyed; at length a bright thought struck him. "I had a boy here last term who could have done that," he said; "there he is now; come up to the blackboard now, Willy Howe, and keep up the honor of the school."

Will was taken by surprise—but he was ready. He had naturally gone over the solution of the sum, while the puzzled class was looking at each other in dismay.

Will was not troubled with diffidence or self-consciousness. He did not think of himself or his clothes, but stepped upon the stage, and went up to the blackboard at once. In a few moments he was ready to give forth the answer in clear tones, and explain the process by which it was attained.

"Thank you, Will," said the master, taking him heartily by the hand.

"Good! Good! Well done!" came from many voices among the visitors.

Will's bright face was full of pleasure, as, with a slight bow, he turned to find a place for himself among the boys on the stage. Pick had come in a few moments before, and the brothers met each other face to face. "Wasn't it good I could do it?" said Will, with delight in his eyes.

"It is too mean of you to come here, looking as you do, to make such a show of yourself and disgracing me. Any of the boys could have done the sum, if they had had time given them," said Pick quickly, in a low, bitter tone, and then he turned rapidly away to avoid Willy. Will saw a door near him, and through it he instantly passed, with a swelling heart. It had been little to him to toil day by day, while his brother enjoyed himself, free from care. It had been little to him to be wearing patch upon patch, that Pick might have the best of Amy's scanty store of materials. This he had himself planned, and he had borne it nobly. But to be despised by that brother, and looked on with shame, this was too much for Will's warm affectionate heart.

He almost ran along the street; then bursting into Amy's presence, he exclaimed, "It is too hard! It is too hard! And I won't bear it."

A flood of tears, half-anger and half-grief, checked his utterance.

It was many minutes before Amy's tenderness could soothe him into sufficient calmness for him to tell his story.

A small bright spot appeared, for a moment, in Amy's cheek, as she listened; but it faded as tears moistened her eyes. "We must pray for Pick," she said gently. "The poor boy is going far astray."

"I feel as if I could never see him again! I can't and I won't bear it!" said Will indignantly.

"Are we to have a home full of hatred and quarrels? You can not separate from your brother. God has placed you together—won't you try to be with him in peace?" said Amy pleadingly.

"It's all his own fault; he must look out for the consequences. I have been willing to do any thing for him, and I *did* love him, but I won't bear this."

"Don't say *did* love him. Remember, 'This commandment have we from our Lord, that he who loveth God, loveth his brother also,'" urged Amy.

"He won't let me love him! He doesn't want to be my brother! I can't get over it," said Willy passionately.

"Then I am to have two naughty brothers to bear with and pray for. I shall love you both, and hope yet to have peace in our poor home," said Amy, taking away the arm that she had thrown round Willy, and looking sadly at him.

"No! No! Amy, that shall never be," said Willy, putting the arm again about him. "I will not try you by my wicked anger. I know I am wrong. I felt so excited and unhappy. I could forgive Pick, if I did not have to see him."

"Willy dear, how do you suppose you have looked, for the last half-hour, to the pure, holy, gentle Jesus? This heated, swollen face does not seem like my own dear Willy, even to me. How must it strike the eye of our sinless Saviour! Do you expect Christ to forgive you again, and own you as one of His dear children?"

"O sister Amy! I should be very miserable if He did not forgive me!" said Willy earnestly.

"He will forgive you, darling, forgive you freely, if you are really sorry for all this angry tumult; but remember the conditions, if you from your heart forgive your brother his trespass," continued Amy.

"Yes, yes; I see it now. Jesus is so good, yet He can forgive me; and even if I do think myself a little better than Pick, and I do, yet I ought to forgive him; I mean to try."

"We have none of us much to boast of. We are all unprofitable servants. You will feel that more and more, Willy, as you go on as a Christian, and that will make it easier for you to forgive," said Amy.

Willy looked into his sister's sweet face. Was her humility the secret of her gentle, forgiving spirit? Good as she was, could she think so lowly of herself? What, then, had a hasty-tempered boy like himself to boast of? He would try to be like her. He would strive to forgive, as he hoped to be forgiven. "I will try, sister Amy, I will try to forgive Pick," said Will. His tone was low and tender, and Amy knew then that the victory was won.

The victory was won. Yet Will had to seek the upper room, and plead earnestly for strength to carry out his resolution, before he dared to meet his brother.

Will had the warmest corner beside the stove, when he heard Pick come in. He jumped up to leave it vacant. That was a happy thought. That one kind action was a great help towards true forgiveness.

Pick was out of humor and out of spirits. He had made such intolerable failures in his recitations, that his triumph of the morning was quite forgotten; and as for Will, he had ceased to think of him or his patched clothes.

Pick looked so pale and miserable, that Will's resentment quite vanished, and his frank face was so bright and kindly, that Harriet nestled close to his side, and said, "I am glad you are not cross, Willy. *We* can have a pleasant time, can't we?"

"Yes, we can have a pleasant time, if we do right," whispered Willy, and he felt the truth of what he said.

Anger, envy, selfishness—they are roots of bitterness, springs of misery. Love, patience, cheerfulness—how they make a home happy and grow in a happy home!

CHAPTER X.

An Opening.

THE shadows of the examination day had floated by like summer clouds, and there was sunshine again in Amy's home.

Pick and Harriet were away at school, and Amy was busy with her needle-work in the kitchen.

Will had placed the old couch by the southern window, where the light would fall on her work, and where her dear face might beam on him when he chanced to be busy in the yard.

On this couch Amy was lying, about a week after the examination, when there was a knock at the street-door.

Amy opened the upper half of it, and then stepped back a little to wait for the gentleman standing there to tell his business.

The shutters in the front-room were closed, and as Amy paused, with the darkened room as a background, the gentleman was unconsciously silent for a moment, while he enjoyed the sweet picture.

"This must be sister Amy," he said. "Can I see you a few moments, and Master Willy too? You see I know something about you, though I am a stranger to you."

Amy opened the inhospitable lower half of the door to her little fortress, and politely invited the gentleman to walk in.

"I shall have to take you into the kitchen, sir, as it is warm there," said Amy leading the way, while the stranger followed.

The kitchen! A place of hurry, heat, closeness, and non-appetizing odors, rose to the gentleman's imagination.

Into no such region was he ushered. The small room was light, cheerful, and scrupulously neat. No great joints, no highly-seasoned stews, no fumes of fat, had tainted that pure air. Where the fare was so simple, the usual combination of odors could not offend.

"My business is more particularly with your brother Willy," said the gentleman, taking the offered chair. "Is he at home?"

"He is at home," said Amy half-smiling, as her eye glanced through the small window.

"I should like to see him," said Mr. Alden, following her glance with his own.

"He is just now in a cloud of dust, and hardly fit to see a stranger," said Amy.

Will had made a coal-sifter of his own, and now he was rattling it most vigorously, while the flying ashes filled the air.

"Let me see him as he is. Honest labor is not a thing to be ashamed of," was the answer.

Amy gave a quick knock upon the window, and the coal-sifter was quiet in a moment. The air cleared, and there stood Willy, with his close-fitting cap tied down at the ears, and his whole person covered with an old wrapper of Amy's, that served him as a suit of armor when he went to his daily battle with the cinders and ashes.

It was a droll-looking figure surely. Will's face was so boy-like, so full of character, that it made all the more funny his girlish attire. His first bright, listening look towards sister Amy turned into a merry laugh, as he saw another face beside hers.

"Come in, Willy; the gentleman wants to see you," said Amy, opening the window for an instant.

Cap and wrapper were doffed in a trice, and after a momentary interview with the pump, Will made his appearance in the kitchen.

He looked none the worse for exercise and cold water, nor for the real glow of welcome on his face, as he recognized the stranger.

"I am glad to see you in your own home, Master Willy, and I hope we shall know more of each other. To make a beginning, I must introduce myself as Charles Alden, of the firm of Alden & Co."

"I am glad to know your name, sir. I did not know what to call you, when I thought about you," said Will.

"Then you have thought about me," said Mr. Alden with a smile; "and I have been thinking about you, and asking about you too."

Will's eager eyes were fixed on the stranger as he went on.

"The master at the school speaks in your praise; your neighbor, Mr. Dobbs, the grocer, says he dare trust anything to you. Now, an honest boy is what I have been looking for. I want just such a one for a vacant position in our establishment. How would you like to be 'cash' for us?" said Mr. Alden kindly.

Will looked wildly at Mr. Alden, as he said, "I don't know what that means, sir, but I would like any honest way of earning my living. I should so like to have a regular business."

"What I shall pay you I cannot say. I can tell better when I find out what you can do. Could you begin to-morrow?"

"Yes, sir, that I could," said Will warmly.

Amy looked doubtfully at Will's worn and patched clothing. She could not bear to expose him to unkind remarks among strangers, in the very dress which had so mortified the foolish Pickard. It was Will's only suit now.

"A week hence will do as well," said

Mr. Alden, reading Amy's glance; "and I had better pay down something in advance, in token of our agreement, that you may not escape from your bargain. I think sister Amy is your banker."

Mr. Alden placed a five-dollar note in Amy's hand as he spoke, while Will blushed and said: "You heard me say that, sir, did you? Well, she's a bank worth trusting."

Mr. Alden had marked the exceeding simplicity and the signs of scrupulous economy, in all about him, from the faded and darned calico covering of the old couch, to the faithfully-mended rag-carpet under his feet.

Sister Amy! The stranger understood her cares and anxieties; he guessed her self-denial and patient industry. How he longed to be to her a true and trusted friend in her adversity!

He deemed the advancing of that five-dollar note a happy thought. Advancing he called it, but he mentally resolved that it should never be named in the account of Will's earnings.

Amy held the money abstractedly in her hand. It seemed a monstrous sum in comparison with the small change with which she had recently been familiar. Should she do right in accepting it on an uncertainty? How nicely it would fit up Willy for his new position! That was a great temptation, but perhaps she had better not take it.

"Something might happen to prevent Will's being at his post," she said hesitatingly; "may be I ought not to take this in advance."

"If Will fails me, you shall be my creditor, and I won't be hard upon you," said Mr. Alden smiling, as he rose to take leave.

A little old-fashioned table stood near him; on it laid a small, well-worn Bible. It was Amy's treasure—a gift from her Sunday-school teacher long ago; so Mr. Alden read, as he opened the book.

"I am glad to find such a comforter here," he said. "You know where to look for counsel and support."

Amy's eyes brightened; now indeed she could wholly trust the stranger! She looked up to him with full confidence as she said, "Yes, that book *is* my comfort. We could not do without it; could we, Willy?"

There was no affectation in the
bright responsive glance that flashed
from Willy's eyes.

The three understood each other
now, and the hearty shake of the hand
with which Mr. Alden closed his visit,
was warmly returned by the orphans.

When   fellow-countrymen   meet
in a foreign land, there is real joyous
warmth in their greeting. But poor and
cold is such a feeling compared with
the glow of the heart, the kindling of
spirit with which true Christians join
hands, when they recognize each other
in this world, where they are strangers
and pilgrims.

Amy rejoiced that there was a
promise of regular industry for her dear
brother; but greater was her rejoicing
that his employer was a Christian
man—one who would watch over his
priceless soul, as well as provide him
with daily labor.

CHAPTER XI.

"Cash."

WILL had no difficulty in finding his way to the establishment of that well-known firm, Alden & Co. Although he had been in great haste to get there, he did not seem in equal haste to enter. He looked twice through the shining glass doors, before he touched the knob with his hand.

When at last he did go in, there was no appearance of diffidence in his manner. He had been but concluding on his plan of operations, and was now ready to act. Walking straight up to the first clerk whom he saw, he asked politely if he could see Mr. Alden.

"Mr. Alden has not come in yet," said the clerk, with an indifferent air.

"Then I will wait for him here," said

Will, perching on one of the high stools, and preparing to reconnoiter from this post of observation.

The scene was quite novel and interesting to the boy. Brought up in country-towns, he had never before been within one of the grand dry-goods stores of the eastern city. A kind of world by itself it seemed to him—a place of wonderful elegance and confusing magnitude.

Branching off in all directions from the main apartment, were other rooms, where there was the same display of costly goods, the same murmur of busy trade.

Will had not been long at his point of observation, when his attention was attracted by an occasional rapping on the counter by the clerks, or a loud cry of "Cash! Cash!"

He soon learned that this was a way of summoning some of the lads near his own age, whom he had before noticed going about outside the counters.

This then was to be his business; like them, to go to the desk for change, while the clerks were always in their places.

Will watched the little fellows with

much interest, and was busy following one of them with his eyes as he wound his way to the desk, when a pleasant voice sounded in his ears.

"So you are finding out what you are to do, and making the best of your time in that way," said Mr. Alden.

"Yes, sir," said Will, jumping down from his seat, and making a polite bow.

"Now follow me, and I will give you your post," said Mr. Alden, leading the way to one of the inner rooms. "You are to be 'cash' for this part of the establishment. Move quickly when you are called, and carry your money carefully, and I shall have no fault to find with you," said Mr. Alden. "Now I must leave you. Mr. Wilcox there will answer any questions that you find it necessary to ask. This is Willy Howe, the boy of whom I spoke to you, Mr. Wilcox."

Mr. Wilcox gave Will a searching glance, of which the boy was unconscious, as he was looking at Mr. Alden, while he said earnestly: "I will try to do my duty, sir."

"That is all that can be asked of you," said Mr. Alden, as he turned to walk away.

Will had been so well pleased with the rich shawls, floating silks, and gay plaids, which had caught his eye in the rooms into which he had been able to peep, that he was somewhat disappointed to find himself among the staple goods, where broadcloths and flannels were ranged in dull piles along the shelves.

Will soon discovered that all was not dull in that neat room. Mr. Wilcox was evidently of a lively turn of mind. There was a quick sparkle in his small blue eyes, a crisp curl to his hair, and an unnecessary friskiness in his movements that told of a degree of natural sportiveness, that made his narrow bounds behind the counter a place of confinement for him.

"New at the business, eh, boy?" said Mr. Wilcox, drawing near to Will.

"I never was in such a splendid store before," said Will frankly.

A sudden rapping on a neighboring counter called Will to his business, and he immediately took charge of the strip of paper and the bank-note that were entrusted to him.

When he returned from the desk,

he found Mr. Wilcox engaged with a customer, with whom he seemed not in the least bit amused.

The counter was strewn with various rolls of red flannel, while an old man was peering at them through his spectacles, and squeezing handfuls of the material in his fist, to ascertain its amount of substance.

"This piece is the best for shirts," said Mr. Wilcox, unrolling a new piece.

"I never wear flannel shirts," said the old man tartly.

"How many yards in that piece?" continued the customer, pointing to the smallest roll.

"Somewhere about twenty. I'll tell you in a moment." Mr. Wilcox referred to a bit of paper fastened to the edge of the flannel, and said: "Yes, twenty yards, at two shillings a yard, that would be forty shillings□just five dollars."

The old man turned away suddenly, but in another moment he was back by the counter, now putting his hand protectingly over his pocket, now passing it meditatingly over the flannel.

"May be you'd say four dollars eighty," he said persuasively.

"We don't do it," said Mr. Wilcox, beginning to gather up the pieces, to restore them to the shelves. "We don't fall on our goods."

"Stop! stop! I'll take it. There's the five dollars; and you may just hand it over."

"We'll send it home for you. Where shall I say?" said Mr. Wilcox, taking out his pencil, and preparing to note the address.

The old man made no reply, but taking up the roll of flannel, he started off towards the door. As he did so, his eyes fell on Will, and their recognition was mutual.

"Mr. Dimer! How do you do, sir?" said Will, putting out his hand.

"Boy, I've been looking for you this week. Come to my house to-night," said the old man hurriedly, as he barely touched Will's hand, and then moved on.

Through the long busy day, Will often thought of the interview with Mr. Dimer. The time of the half-yearly payment of interest on the borrowed money had arrived. Had Amy something laid by for this purpose? Will tried not to dwell on this question, but it would thrust itself into his mind.

"Money! Why, it is poured out here like dust. A little would not be missed," so whispered the tempter at his heart. A bank-note was in Will's hand; did he listen to the tempter? "Resist the devil and he will flee from you!" says the holy Scripture.

Will did resist him then with indignant scorn, and with his second thought to pray, "Lord, help me to do right: lead me not into temptation: deliver me from evil."

How much Will had to tell Amy that evening at supper, when the day was fairly done! He felt as if he had had the first peep at the world, its vanities, and its temptations. The meeting with Mr. Dimer was not forgotten. Amy's calm look, when it was mentioned, assured Will that here he had nothing to fear.

Amy had not let her pride in her brother lead her to foolish extravagance. The neat, coarse suit she had bought for him had not touched upon her private store, for sudden necessities had not even consumed Mr. Alden's five dollars.

"How wonderful it is that all our needs are supplied," said Amy, as she drew out her small purse. "I am never anxious now. It seems to me that the poor ought to love God better than the rich."

"Why, Amy?" said Will earnestly; his day's experience had made him feel poorer than usual.

"Because God seems so very near to us, helping us in all our difficulties, and providing as it were directly for us. He seems so really our Father, on whom we depend," said Amy earnestly.

"I love to hear you say so, Amy," said Will warmly. "I saw so many things to-day, I wanted for you; and I thought how nicely I could fix you up; and I almost wanted to be rich. I am afraid I coveted."

"Don't covet anything for my sake, Willy," said Amy affectionately. "My dear, kind brother is better to me than great riches. Fine clothing would not suit my poor body. I have that temptation removed from me. Dear Willy, I am quite content. I love to lean on God, and trust the future to Him."

Willy looked long and lovingly into Amy's sweet, placid face. Yes, there was content there—true peace; this world could not add to her joy!

CHAPTER XII.

Darkness.

$\mathcal{I}$T was a pleasure to walk along the lighted streets, and peep in at the bright windows, but now he did not suffer himself to stop even to linger at the print-shops, but went straight on his course to Mr. Dimer's. He was out on business, and must not dilly-dally. Mr. Dimer was on the door-step—could he be watching for him?

"Here you are. I was just going to close up. As it is, I've put out the gas in the front-shop; it was only wasting itself. Come in here," said the old pawnbroker.

The spot to which he led the way was not tempting, and a timid boy might have hesitated to enter, but Will was troubled with no such difficulties.

A sort of back-shed had been shut in and plastered; and here was plainly the old man's abode. The small, narrow bed, the single old table, bearing its one plate and cup and saucer, told of the home and habits of the pawnbroker.

"Sit down, boy. May be you'd forgot your half-year was up?" said the old man keenly.

"I had, but sister Amy hadn't. She knew the very day. She says its right to be exact about business matters," said Will.

"Yes, that's right, sure enough," was the approving answer.

"Twenty-five dollars, at seven per cent, for half a year, that is just eighty-seven and a half cents, as I make it," said Will laying the sum down on the table.

The old man took hold of it eagerly, and then producing a quit-book, made a minute of the payment, and at the same time gave Will a receipt for the sum paid.

The boy rose to go, but the old man detained him, saying, "Child, sit down. Are you afraid to stay a minute with an old man, who has nobody to speak to, when he's aching to talk over some things he knows of?"

"You must lead a lonely life," said Will kindly, as he resumed his seat.

"No matter about that, now!" was the short answer. "Here's what I want to see you about—this flannel," and the old man pointed to the roll in the corner, "this flannel, I say, is for the poor. Five dollars I paid for it; yet I am going to give it away. I want you to take it to the ladies that take in poor children, and train 'em up right. Their place is only two blocks off—that's the right thing, take 'em young, before they get in bad ways. It's not easy teaching old dogs new tricks! Will you do it, boy?"

"That I will, gladly."

Will was again rising as he spoke, but with an impatient gesture, the old man motioned him to sit down—and then went on, "It's for the poor, you see, but I want to do it on the sly; they say that's the right way. I han't never been dishonest, exactly—I han't never received no goods as I knew was stolen; but somehow I feel as if I'd better be doin' now, to wipe my old scores out."

"I don't quite understand you, sir," said Will frankly.

"A body can't live forever! I'm almost worn out," said the old man quickly. "There was words in that big old book of yours that set me to thinkin' of that, pretty steady. You see I an't one of the 'jewels'—the 'oven' is more like for me, when my time comes. *'And the day that cometh shall burn them up, saith the Lord of hosts, that it shall leave them neither root nor branch.'*"

These last words were spoken in low trembling tones that chilled Will's young blood, and he was silent.

"Yes, boy," Mr. Dimer continued, after a pause; "yes, the likes of me had better be settlin' up with Providence. Five dollars the flannel cost me. You take it to the ladies. They are doin' the right thing—and, may be, I'll get a share of the blessing."

"God gives us fully, without our doing any thing; you know that, sir," said Will modestly.

"I don't know any such thing! I don't feel it here!" said the old man, laying his hand on his heart.

"But Jesus suffered and died for us, that we might go free, and be happy with Him in heaven," said Will earnestly.

"What wouldn't I give to be a boy again, and take that in, just where I want it! It's no use now! I've been sowin' all my life, and the reapin' time is coming, soon—it is here! O child! Thank God that you've found Him now! It's hard work gropin' after Him with worn wicked hands!"

"Jesus can help you," said Will affectionately.

"I don't know Him! He don't know me! I never tried to know Him when I was young. He don't want my poor old tagged-out life. I an't worth any thing for Him, now."

"Have you got a Bible, that tells about Jesus?" said Will earnestly.

"Yes, yes, I bought one, and opened it too. I read: *'The wicked shall be turned into hell, and all the people that forget God.'* There it was, plain as print. There's nothing for me now, but just to do what I can to make up, and may be get off easier for that."

Poor Will! Teaching others was a new business for him. How he longed for sister Amy's sweet, wise, persuasive words, to comfort and guide the sin-sick old man.

"Read about Jesus, and you'll understand it all then. Ask Him to help you, and it will be all right by and by," said Will.

"Never! There's nothing right for me! Go, boy—go on your errand. Go and be thankful you are not like me, too old, too bad to take in the best religion the Bible ever preached! Go!"

The last word was said imperatively, and Will hastened to obey.

"Round the corner there, No. 75," said the pawnbroker in more softened tones, as he handed Will the roll of flannel. "Round the corner there. There's no word to be left with it, only an old Sinner sends it, and says to the ladies, teach the children right when they are young." The door closed suddenly, and Will stood in the street. He delivered the message as it was given to him, and then walked thoughtfully homeward.

"'Tis easier far, if we begin
To serve the Lord betimes,
For sinners who grow old in sin,
Are hardened by their crimes."

These lines Will had learned long ago, but now they came to his mind in full force; from his heart he thanked God that he had early learned to love Him, and earnestly he prayed that he might so live, that old age might find him longing to go to his well-known Saviour, rather than groping after that Heavenly Friend, long forgotten and despised.

CHAPTER XIII.

A New Care.

*S*OME weeks had passed since the events related in the last chapter. Will had become accustomed to his new occupation, and was already a favorite throughout the establishment.

"Come, 'Cash,'" said Mr. Alden playfully one evening, "I am going home now, and I want you to bear me company."

Will was delighted at the proposition. A walk with Mr. Alden was always a source of true enjoyment to him.

Mr. Alden had the faculty which only belongs to lovers of the young— that of gaining their confidence, and putting them perfectly at ease.

Once in the open air, Will ceased to look upon Mr. Alden as his employer, but chatted along in his own bright, glad way.

They had not gone far, when Mr. Alden said, "Will, I hope you are not getting into trouble. I saw you coming out of a pawnbroker's shop the other day." The remark was accompanied by an anxious, searching look.

"That was only a friendly visit," said Will soberly.

"A friendly visit! How did you make such an acquaintance?"

Frankly, and in a few words, Will told the story of his first meeting with Mr. Dimer, and then passed on to his present sad state of mind. "I wish you knew him, sir. You could talk to him better than I can."

"I will know him—that is, if he will let me," said Mr. Alden.

"Thank you! Thank you!" said Will, as warmly as if some favor had been promised to himself. At this moment they were passing a theatre, whose wide entrance was brilliantly lighted and already thronged. In that entrance Will saw something that made him start, and stop for a moment.

Two lads were just going in. He

could not be mistaken in that tall, slender figure, that light curling hair. Yet the dress was not the same. Pick had no such fashionable suit.

"What is the matter, Will? What do you see?" asked Mr. Alden.

"I thought I saw a friend; but I must have been mistaken. It could not be," said Will thoughtfully.

There was no more pleasant chat for Will that evening; the figure entering the theatre was before him through all his walk, and when he saw Pick's place at the tea-table vacant, he became still more anxious and puzzled.

Pick's irregularity at meals was so frequent, that Amy was not particularly troubled by this instance of it.

The kind sister knew full well that Pick was in temptation, if not already walking in an evil way. The books he read at the fireside showed a tainted taste. The company he kept could do him no good. There was a wild, reckless way abut him, that boded evil. His evenings were rarely passed at home, while he roundly refused to say where he spent his time, declaring himself to be his own master, and not bound to account for his doings to any woman.

Was not this a trouble that was to rob Amy of her peaceful calm?

Amy had a Friend who is powerful to move the hearts of men, as well as to govern and guide the universe. To this Friend she prayed. On Him she cast even this, her greatest care. He could watch over and reclaim the erring brother. It is written: *"With God all things are possible."*

CHAPTER XIV.

Christmas Eve.

CHRISTMAS had come, the second Christmas that the little Howes had spent in their queer, old-fashioned home.

One capacious little stocking was hung by the kitchen fire-place. Harriet had left it there in full faith that somehow and by somebody it would be filled.

"Put the apple in the toe, Will," said Amy; "that will fill it out to begin with."

"Yes; but let me drop in the five-cent piece first. It will please Harriet so to find it there," said Will, suiting the action to the word.

Amy's own dear little Bible next went in—her gift to Harriet—with many prayers. Gladly would she have placed in its stead a bright New Testament, but Amy gave of what she had with a loving spirit.

A large-eyed rag-doll thoroughly filled the whole half of the stocking, and its flat face looked out complacently on the world from the top. Hanging beside the stocking, Will put a little wagon of his own manufacture—a suitable vehicle for Miss Dolly to ride out in, being, like herself, more substantial than beautiful, and moreover of domestic origin.

Amy and Will surveyed with satisfaction the result of their labors, and then sat down with smiling faces.

At that moment a knock was heard at the door. Will ran to open it, and came back with his face beaming. "It was Mr. Alden's own porter," he said. "What can be in the box—it is very heavy."

The box which had been handed him was only four inches square. A more experienced eye than Will's would have guessed at once what it contained.

It did not take many minutes to open it. "It is father's watch!" exclaimed Amy. There could be no mistake; there was the inscription: "George Howe."

Will had not stopped to read that inscription; he was deep in a note addressed to "Master William Howe," which lay in the bottom of the box. The note was as follows:

DEAR LITTLE 'CASH':

I send your father's watch as a reward for your faithful industry. Mr. Dimer has no further claims upon it. I have seen the poor man several times lately. With him all is gloom. Would that at this blessed time Christ might be born for him.

Wishing you and sister Amy a very happy Christmas, I am your true friend,

CHARLES ALDEN.

"Hear!" said Will, reading the note aloud. "Is not that like Mr. Alden? So generous! So good! So kind! What a long time it seems, Amy, since I went out that door with this watch in my hand! Why, I feel at least five years older."

"You are not wrinkled yet," said Amy fondly.

"I never mean to be; that is, I don't mean to have my face all knit up

by business cares, and cross scowls.
There's Mr. Alden, he is always busy,
and he has such great concerns to attend to, but he never seems hurried and
worried. He's like you, Amy, in that."

"Like me!" said Amy, smiling. Amy's
brow did cloud up suddenly at that
very moment, but it was but a passing shadow driven away by the sweet
sunshine.

There was a sound of singing along
the street, and then Pick came in. He
looked flushed and excited, and was going directly up-stairs, when Will called
out, "See here, Pick; see Mr. Alden's
note, and the watch, and just take one
look at Harriet's stocking."

Pick gave one glance at the note, and
then threw it down; a significant smile
crossed his face as he took the watch in
his hand, but at Harriet's stocking he
did not resign to look.

Without speaking a word, Pick
mounted the stairs, and the creaking of
his bed was soon heard. Pick's evening
prayers had long since been given up.

Amy and Will were silent for a moment. Then the sister said, "You are
such a comfort to me, Will."

"Pick—" began Will impatiently.

"We must pray for Pick," said Amy tenderly, and she knelt down as she spoke.

Will knelt at her side, and then there went up such prayer as angels love to hear.

There was a stealthy step on the stairs, and the door leading to the upper rooms was quietly closed. Pick could not hear that prayer unmoved; he would shut out its sound, lest he should be led to repentance and a better life.

CHAPTER XV.

Not a Merry Christmas.

HARRIET was not a child to oversleep herself on Christmas morning. With the first gray streak of dawn she was awake, and soon she bore off her stocking to bed, as a mouse takes his treasure to his hiding-place. Her merry shouts put an end to all further dozing for the household at once—they must rouse up, and have "merry" Christmas whether they would or not.

"I wonder what time it is," thought Will, and in the dimness he reached out his hand to find the watch he had placed at his bedside. It was not there! "Why, Pick! Where can it be!" said Will turning to speak to his brother—but his brother too, was gone!

Will's first impulse was to call

Amy, but a second and more unselfish thought prevailed. He would not worry her about what might be a mere trick of Pick's, a mere plan to annoy him.

"Pick is late to-day," said Amy, as she took her seat at the breakfast-table. "I had hoped to have you all together, on Christmas morning."

"It is a great deal pleasanter without Pick!" said Harriet, putting her new doll in the vacant chair. "My Georgiana won't say anything cross to anybody."

"Hush, Harriet dear," said Amy gently, as she stepped to the stairway—"Pick, Pick! Wake up, Pick—I want you all here this morning." Amy's voice sounded pleasantly up the stairway, but there was no reply.

"I'll give him a cold water waking," said Harriet, seizing a mug of water and rushing past Amy up the stairs. She returned as quickly, and with her eyes round with astonishment, she exclaimed, "Pick is not there! Did you know it, Willy?"

"Pick must have risen very early," said Willy. "He was gone when I woke. I did not say any thing about it, for I thought it was perhaps some joke of his, and he would come in while we were at breakfast."

That was not a merry Christmas day to the little Howes. A few of Pick's better articles of clothing were found to be missing, and this, in addition to his secret disappearance, convinced both Amy and Will that he was not merely gone for a single day.

Of the watch Will said nothing; that sorrow he hid in his heart—he would not believe that Pick had taken it. It might yet be found, where he had mischievously secreted it.

It was hard for Will to show his usual activity, when he appeared the next day at his post. "Cash is out of humor at last!" said Mr. Wilcox playfully—"Christmas did not agree with him. Cash is very cross," he continued. "Wouldn't smile. No, not on any account," and Mr. Wilcox drew his own face into an expression of mock solemnity.

"I have had trouble at home," said Will, tears rushing to his eyes.

"Cash! Cash!" The call was in Willy's ears, and he had to obey. Through the long day he went about with a heavy heart. At noon, no news from Pick; at

evening, the same sad answer to the
question that burst from his lips, as
soon as he entered his home. The next
morning brought a letter addressed to
Mr. William Howe, in Pick's well-known
hand. It began:

*You have been wanting to be the
oldest, Will, and now you can have
your way. I am off the track; when
you receive this, I shall be on my
way to England. You may be proud
to claim me some day. I don't know
whether I shall own my relation-
ship to my clod-hopping, counter-
jumping brother. I am going on to
the stage, a position for which my
talents fit me. Our troupe has an en-
gagement in London, so you see that
gives me a chance to see something
of the world. When you receive this,
I shall be on the ocean.*

*Father's watch, I have taken
possession of. It came home in good
time. Being the older brother, I have
the best right to it.*

*I owe some little bills about
town, that I know you will be too
honorable to leave unpaid. I have*

ordered them to be sent in to you, on the first of January.

I dare say you will all be glad to have me out of the way, all but Amy. I do believe she cares something for me.

Your Brother,
PICKARD HOWE.

Pick could not have doubted Amy's love for him, if he had seen her look of anguish, as Will read this letter aloud. She bowed her head upon her hands, in silence, and her tears flowed fast. As it is always with true affection, excuses for him poured into her mind. "The poor boy has never known a mother's care; he has inherited his father's wild, roving spirit; he is following his father's example. Who knows what he might have been in a different home! May God watch over him, and deliver him from evil!" So thought Amy, and so she prayed, while her tears fell fast.

Will walked the room, conflicting emotions struggling in his mind. Indignation and sorrow, love and scorn, by turns had the mastery. Pick had never seemed so dear, yet, never so despised; the brother's warm affection was roused by the sudden separation, yet the manner of that separation kindled most contrary feelings.

"Poor Pick!" he said at length, "Poor Pick, he has chosen a hard lot. How I pity him!" Will's better self had triumphed. With Amy he could now weep for the wanderer; with her he could pray that he might, like the prodigal, be brought repentant to his home.

CHAPTER XVI.

Little Harriet.

ICK'S debts proved by no means the trifling affairs of which he had spoken. Will's forgiveness was not to be a mere matter of momentary feeling; it was to be shown in a long course of self-denial. To pay for the indulgences in dress that Pick had allowed himself for his evenings abroad, Will must toil, and Amy must save and mend and plan and think, to economize, when economy seemed to have reached its utmost verge.

Will and Amy were helping each other; that was a support to both.

Hard thoughts of Pick were checked, when Will saw Amy's uncomplaining patience. Will's cheerful aid made Amy's labor lighter. God has made it a pleasure for human beings to join together in good works. Sympathy is pleasant everywhere, but it is chiefly precious on the heavenly path.

Harriet was not particularly well pleased with the new state of things introduced into the household by Pick's departure. That departure she considered a welcome relief, and she had hoped that it would be followed by a time of unwonted cheerfulness in the establishment.

She chafed not a little at the new system of patching and saving, and by her unreasonable spirit added greatly to Amy's cares.

She could not see that the same selfishness was working in her that had reached such a despicable excess in her absent brother. "If I have to wear that big patch on the front of my cloak, I won't go to school," she said angrily one morning.

"I am sorry you tore it yesterday. I have mended it as well as I can," said Amy gently. "We have to be very careful now, you know."

"I don't see what we have to do with old Pick's debts," said Harriet sharply. "I don't want to be scrimped for his foolishness."

Much as Harriet had disliked Pick's conduct, his silly pride and his rudeness to his sister had had their influence. Ah! That is the danger of evil companions; we hate their sin, yet learn unconsciously to imitate it!

"Harriet! Dear Harriet!" said Amy reproachfully.

Harriet threw her arms round Amy's neck, and gave her half-a-dozen kisses. She was sorry to see Amy grieved, not sorry for her fault.

Harriet hurried off to school, while Amy was attending to household matters. The despised warm cloak was left at home, while a thin shawl was substituted in its place.

Amy had no sleep that night; Harriet was tossing restlessly, now asking in husky tones for water, and now half-delirious with fever. The sudden violent cold which she had taken would not yield to the simple means that Amy used. As the day wore on, it was plain that Harriet was growing rapidly worse, and at noon Will was dispatched for a physician.

Dr. Brooks shook his head gravely, and returned at evening to see the little patient again.

Then came days and nights when Amy seemed to have but one thought and one aim. Her own weakness, her very pains were unnoticed, while she ministered by the sick-bed, with all the loving tenderness of a mother.

The scanty purse poured forth its contents, as freely as if it were a golden mine. What the suffering child needed, she must have, though the future should be filled with thronging cares.

Three weeks had passed since the lively, active Harriet had been transformed into a poor fever-tossed being, without power to say a cheerful word, or give a kindly, natural smile. Now she was for the first time in a quiet sleep. Amy stepped softly to the bureau, and taking out her worn pocket-book, satisfied herself that not even a stray piece of change was lurking in its folds. What was to be done? A whole week must elapse before the day of Will's monthly payment. In the meantime how was the little family to be provided with the mere necessaries of life?

Amy's embroidery had been laid aside; she had no time to renew it now; without undertaking additional labor, she feared that she should sink under the unwonted fatigue she was undergoing. Already, every movement was pain, and weary limbs and aching back might at any time utterly give way. For the first time, Amy was thoroughly disheartened. It is hard for the spirit to bear up when the body has been too sorely taxed. Anxious, long-protracted watching by the bed of sickness wears upon the strongest nerves. What wonder then, that Amy's feeble exhausted frame now clogged and bore down her heaven-taught spirit?

Weak, lonely, helpless, the poor lame girl felt, as she looked now at the dear little sufferer in the bed, and now at the empty pocket-book beside her. Tears, hot tears burst from her eyes, and for a moment all seemed darkness.

A footstep below roused Amy, and she stepped cautiously down to give Will the simple lunch prepared for him—dinner the meal was still called, though it had lately become but the poorest representation of that comfortable repast.

"What is the matter, Amy? Is Harriet worse?" said Will anxiously, as he noticed on his sister's face the signs of recent tears.

"No; thank God, Harriet is better. I think! I believe I am feeling a little re-action at the relief, after being so long anxious about her and—"

"And what, Amy?" said Will eagerly.

"And I don't know what we are to do now," said Amy, the tears again filling her eyes. "I am weak and foolish, Will," she said, as he put his arm round her and looked up anxiously into her face. "It is only that the pocket-book is empty, and I don't exactly see what we are to do until next week."

"I might ask Mr. Alden to advance me," said Will thoughtfully. "He came home to-day, and I am sure he would do it willingly. He would think we had been extravagant, I know, but I could not tell him about Pick."

"No, no!" said Amy. "We must keep poor Pick's secret. But Will, your payments only cover what we absolutely need. If we take in advance now, we shall be as badly off next month. There will be the doctor to pay, and Harriet will need a great many things to make her comfortable, as she is getting well. If there was only something I could do!"

"You have done too much already, and you are quite worn out," said Will tenderly. "I am the one that ought to take care of you, and I have tried," and a blank look of helpless disappointment came over the poor boy's face.

He had tried his best, and now he seemed about to fail and to see "poverty come in like an armed man," in spite of his industry. Will's manliness forsook him, and he bowed his head to hide his tears. This was just what Amy needed; her courage and her faith returned to her at once.

"Cheer up, Will," she said in her own sweet tones. "Cheer up, I have been setting a bad example. We have no right to despair; with such a Heavenly Father to depend upon, we have nothing to fear. Draw up to the table, Mr. Howe. Will you have some of the roast-beef? Cut a piece for yourself. There, a slice of bread, a few tomatoes, and some of this mashed potato to go with them!"

Amy spoke playfully as she pushed the single loaf of bread on the table towards Will, and pretended at the same time to help him to the various articles mentioned.

There was no bitterness in her manner, and Will smiled in spite of himself, as she did the honors for him. Cheerfulness was natural to Will, and in a few moments he was talking as brightly and hopefully as if he had not a care in the world.

"Keep up your courage, Amy," he said as he went out of the door. "Keep up your courage. Who knows what good thing may be in store for us all?"

Amy returned to the sick-room's depressing atmosphere, while Will went forth into the clear fresh air. He had not gone far, when he met Mr. Alden.

"A little late, are you not, Will?" said the employer. "How have you been getting on since I have been gone? You have not fallen into irregular ways, I hope."

"I haven't been quite as regular as usual, sir," said Will frankly. "My little sister has been very sick, and Amy has had a great deal to do, and I have stopped sometimes to help her a little. I thought you would excuse it, when you knew my reason."

"And so I do, willingly," said Mr. Alden; "but now, we must not stop here talking while Mr. Wilcox may be drumming on the counter, and calling out 'Cash,' as if he could make you hear at this distance." Mr. Alden passed on.

"Perhaps he will look in upon Amy, just to say a kind word, now he knows we have sickness," thought Will, and he turned his head to see if his employer did not enter the old double-door.

CHAPTER XVII.

A Friend.

WHEN Harriet woke up from her long nap, she was evidently better. Her eyes had something of their own natural expression, and the hand that Amy took in hers no longer throbbed and thrilled like a frightened bird.

Amy bent lovingly down, and kissed the child as she said, "You are better, darling, and I am so glad."

"I want fresh water," said Harriet languidly, as she moved her dry lips.

"I will get you some," said Amy, going as cheerfully down-stairs as if every step had not cost her pain.

At that moment the outer-door silently opened, and when Amy reached the lower room, a stranger was standing before her. That was no face from which to start and turn away, though met in the midst of one's home.

The lady was simply dressed, but there was about her an air of refinement that could not be mistaken. Her oval face was smooth and soft as a child's, but there was in it a wisdom and a wealth of kindliness that only well-spent years can give. Now, that face was beaming with a tender, motherly expression that accorded well with the stranger's words and actions.

"Poor dear!" she said as she took both Amy's hand in hers. "I wish I had been with you before!"

The marks of patient, exhausting watching were too plainly written in Amy's face to escape even a careless glance.

"I have come to help you now. I am Mrs. Alden, and I know all about Will and sister Amy! Shall I put my bonnet down here, before I go up-stairs?"

There was help, real loving help in the stranger's face and manner, and Amy knew it.

"Thank you, thank you, ma'am!" Amy tried to say, but the tears would come instead. Poor Amy! She was quite worn out.

"Dear child!" said Mrs. Alden, putting her arm tenderly round the orphan girl, and pressing her to her affectionate bosom. "Dear child!" she said no more, but Amy felt comforted.

Amy went for the cold water; and when she returned to Harriet's bedside, she found Mrs. Alden sitting there, as calmly and quietly as if she were at home.

Harriet liked strangers; and now she had Mrs. Alden's tapering hand in hers, and was pushing the wedding-ring up and down on her slender finger.

"Now, Amy, dear, you go and take a good rest, while I stay with the little patient. She and I will get on nicely, won't we?" and Mrs. Alden turned towards the child such a sweet, smiling face, that she could not help bowing her head in assent.

Amy did go to the next room, but it was to pray before she slept. She had a thanksgiving to pour out to the ever-watchful Heavenly Father, who had sent her such a friend in her hour of need. The empty pocket-book was forgotten. Amy could leave all now in the Providential Hand.

Such sleep as Amy enjoyed! Those only who have known weeks of weary watching, can have any idea of such sound, dreamless sleep. It was dusk in the little low room when Amy opened her eyes. She started up and hastened to Harriet's bedside.

There the sweet, motherly face greeted her like a blessing.

"The doctor has been here, and he says our little patient is better, and we may begin to give her nourishment now. A little beef-tea given to her frequently, he thinks, would be best for her," said Mrs. Alden cheerfully.

A blank, troubled look floated across Amy's face for an instant.

"If you will sit here a little while now, dear, I will go and get my supper; and when I come back, I will bring the beef-tea. I know just how it should be made. There is quite an art about it, I assure you."

"You are very kind!" was all Amy could say, as she took the vacant seat pointed out to her.

"She could not have read my thoughts. She little knows what it is to have an empty purse and a sick sister!"

said Amy to herself, as Mrs. Alden left the house.

Mrs. Alden could not have read Amy's thoughts without some previous assistance. Several trifles had been wanted from the lower room, while Amy was sleeping, and Mrs. Alden, expecting to be henceforward the nurse, had no hesitation about familiarizing herself with her field of labors. She saw that Harriet was now to need nourishment, and she had vague ideas of preparing for her a little panda, a buttered benjamin, or a few spoonfuls of broth. The materials even for such simple diet were not to be found in Amy's empty larder.

The few dishes on the shelf were scrupulously clean—painfully clean—they seemed so little familiar with food. The few loaves of wholesome bread that were folded in the snow-white towel, were the only signs that Will and Amy ever thought of eating at all. There could be but one reason for such a state of things, and Mrs. Alden's motherly heart throbbed painfully as she thought of the plenty that had reigned in her home, while poverty had so tried the industrious orphans.

It is the industrious, respectable people in humble life, who often suffer most from want. They shrink from the exposure that is a little thing to the street-beggar, or the well-known pensioners upon the wealthy.

Poor and rich should know each other as friends; then in the hour of need, it is comparatively easy for the unfortunate to accept aid from those whom they love, and who have guessed at their necessities.

Mrs. Alden blamed herself for the false delicacy which had kept her from intruding into Amy's home. She had been wanted there, she saw, and she meant to make full amends for the past.

When Mrs. Alden returned, it was to pass the night at the Howes'. She had brought her wrapper, she said, and some trifles in the basket that Mr. Alden had carried for her. There was the beef-tea, the very essence of the nutritious meat, brown, and just salted to suit the taste. Amy and Will were both at the bed-side, to see Harriet take the first mouthful. She swallowed it eagerly as a starved child, and opened her lips for more.

"Presently, darling. That will do for the first time," said Mrs. Alden gently, and Harriet quietly submitted.

Here was another difficulty removed from Amy's path. Harriet was willful in health, and since her sickness had been by no means submissive to Amy's authority. Amy had wondered how she could persuade Harriet into the obedience to orders that would be all-important for her restoration to health. A sister who governs only by moral persuasion, always has her own difficulties.

Mrs. Alden did not drive Amy altogether from the sick-room. She let her busy herself about Harriet; but when ten o'clock came, she said decidedly, "Now, Amy, dear, I am going to bid you good-night; you need not hurry up to get breakfast; you will find a cold chicken and some other little things I put in the basket. You ought not to be troubled with cooking when there is so much to do in the house. People must help each other when sickness comes."

Could Mrs. Alden have guessed her secret? Amy thought not. Mrs. Alden's manner was so free and natural. At any rate she would stifle every feeling of pride, and be thankful for the kindly supplies.

It was vain for Amy to plead that she had had a good rest, and was no longer sleepy. Mrs. Alden gently laid her hand over her lips and said, "I am going to take care of you too, dear Amy, just like a mother. You are not too old to obey, my child. I know whose back is tired out, and who needs quiet, if she does not need sleep."

Mrs. Alden removed her hand and put a kiss in its place—a kiss which Amy cordially returned. She could not help loving Mrs. Alden, and obeying her too; there was decision about the good lady, as well as gentleness.

Will and Amy unpacked the basket together, before they parted for the night.

"Take a lunch now, Will," said Amy, as she saw him giving loving looks at the cold ham and snowy biscuits that accompanied the chicken.

"I believe I will," said the brother;

and it was plain how his boyish appetite had suffered, so hearty was the zest with which he made way with the good cheer.

"He feedeth the ravens when they cry," said Amy, looking earnestly into Will's face. "We were too anxious, too distrustful to-day, Will."

"We were, Amy. I felt as if I should die when I saw you giving up," said the brother.

"We will ask forgiveness and send up our thanksgiving at the same time," said Amy. Together they knelt, and together they rose after their true prayer, their true communion with their Heavenly Father.

"Now, go right to sleep, Amy. You can feel easy to leave Harriet with such a good, experienced nurse," said Will.

"She is very, very kind, and she knows so much about sickness. I begin to love her already," answered Amy.

"And so do I," said Will. "I love her because she is so good to Harriet; but I am best pleased because she is going to take care of you, sister Amy. You are always thinking of others, and forgetting yourself."

"Nonsense, Will!" said Amy smiling, as she bade him good-night.

Will had spoken the truth. Amy was always thinking of others, and now she was really so worn out, she needed someone to think of her. Mrs. Alden's warm, motherly ways were a perfect cordial to the weary girl; there was rest to her in the thought of that kind, wise friend so near at hand.

Verily, God had remembered His promises to the orphan, when He sent Mrs. Alden to cheer Amy with her hearty kindliness.

CHAPTER XVIII.

Sunshine.

THE week that Amy had so much dreaded, fleeted by like the happy days of childhood. A sudden brightness seemed shed abroad in Amy's home.

Harriet was gaining steadily. One morning she was bolstered up with the pillows to take her breakfast; the next, Mrs. Alden held her in her kind arms; each little sign of returning health was welcomed and rejoiced over, as parents note the pretty baby ways, by which the unconscious infant becomes the dear, loving, playful little child.

Mrs. Alden was true to her promise. She cared for Amy as well as for Harriet. She had ever an excuse for that basket of good cheer, that was sure to arrive every morning. Amy was worn out, and her strength must not be taxed with household cares. She had to help nurse a little yet, and that was quite enough for her, the true friend would say. So delicately and kindly did Mrs. Alden manage to see the orphans made for the time comfortable; but she was not satisfied with that.

Happy is it when husband and wife share the same loving, liberal spirit; so is their own fireside made glad with a gladness that reaches many humble homes, that were otherwise dark and dreary.

In planning deeds of thoughtful kindness, Mr. and Mrs. Alden had passed many pleasant hours. He loved to see her face glow with tender, generous interest in the unfortunate. He loved to see her ministering to the afflicted, with the gentleness and delicacy that can only come from the purest sympathy. It was her joy to note his large-hearted spirit, and to hear him speak of far-reaching plans of benevolence, to which he lent his substantial aid, while he was none the less mindful of the many claims for help about his daily path.

Willy Howe's pay-day was a day of

rejoicing to him, and of devout gratitude to Amy.

Mr. Alden knew that Willy was performing a man's part for his orphan sisters, and with a manly spirit was laboring for them, and he well thought it became the noble brother to win a man's earnings.

Mr. Alden was not a person who feared to depart from his usual routine, lest evil should follow. What his heart prompted and his judgment approved, he did, let who would criticize or object.

He lent his aid to the orphan Howes in a way that he would relieve them from a burden of obligation, while it freed them from the fear of want.

Will's honest efforts were crowned with success. A regular clerkship was given him, and a regular salary, which, in Amy's hands, would insure comfort in their modest home.

Harriet needed fresh air—pure air outside the city's bounds, Mrs. Alden said. She must have a daily drive, and Amy must not speak of staying at home to do "that mending." Both must go. Mrs. Alden must see them both look plump and rosy.

Amy smiled, and she could not refuse. How she did enjoy seeing once more green fields like those that had formerly been so dear to her. How Harriet rejoiced to point out the wild flowers springing in the woods, and the forest-trees putting forth their leaves.

That drive was a daily joy, a kind of drawing near to the Great Creator; it seemed to Amy a clear view of her faithful Heavenly Friend. With the arching sky above her, and wide-spreading fields about her, she realized more fully that the God who made the universe was yet her own dear Lord, in whom she put her trust.

Other pleasures too were becoming known at the Howe's. Young faces looked in on their way to school, "to see the little girl mamma had been nursing," or to bring her some pretty book to read, or a new doll, with which to amuse herself when she was weary.

Then there were Mr. Dimer's frequent calls, now to bring an orange for Harriet, now to ask Will to do a bit of writing for him in the evening. An excuse the old man always found, yet there were ever two hidden motives for his visits. He wanted to do some kindly action, he wanted to have one more glance at the peace and purity of a Christian home, where Jesus was loved and trusted.

And was Harriet made more spoiled and willful by all the kindness showered on her?

Take a peep at the sisters after their return from one of their drives. Harriet is lying on the couch, while Amy sits beside her.

The little girl looks up tenderly into her sister's face and says, "Everybody is so kind to me, and I am so ashamed. Kiss me, sister Amy, and tell me you forgive me all my naughty ways. I don't want to do wrong any more; indeed I don't. I have asked God to forgive me, and now if you will kiss me, and say you forgive me too, I shall be so happy."

Happy Amy! Happy Harriet! Happy angels rejoicing in heaven!

CHAPTER XIX.

Will's Place.

THE long years go by, and where is our orphan boy?

"So you are twenty-one to-day, Will," said Mr. Wilcox, laughing, "and you have been buying a new house, and all manner of nice things. There's a lady in the case, I dare say," and Mr. Wilcox gave a wonderfully roguish look as he spoke.

Willy Howe had a roguish glance too in his eye, as he answered, "Yes, you are right there; there is a lady in the case."

"And a pretty one too, I'll warrant," continued Mr. Wilcox.

"Just the kind of face I fancy," said Will with a smile.

"You mean to make her comfortable, that's plain. Take care you don't spoil her!" was the reply.

"She can't be spoiled. If you only knew her!" said Will warmly.

"Perhaps you have bought the long-wished-for yellow-satin couch," said Mr. Alden, who happened to hear the conversation.

"Not exactly! But you are in my secret," said Will.

"Yes, and endorse your sentiments. She can't be spoiled. There is that about her that will keep her safe, until she is gathered among the jewels 'that shall shine forever,'" said Mr. Alden.

Yes, for Amy, Will was enjoying fitting up his new home. The land on which the old house stood had become every year more valuable. It was sold at last, and Will bought a neat, pleasant home for his sisters on the outskirts of the city. Harriet's comfort was not forgotten; but sister Amy was chiefly in Will's thoughts. Dear sister Amy! He longed to reward her for all her years of patient, unselfish kindness.

She had now her brother's arm to lean upon, her brother's prosperity to rejoice in; and he longed to see her in such a home as he felt she would adore.

CHAPTER XX.

Family Scenes.

THERE was no foolish luxury in Willy Howe's new home. He had known what it was to struggle with want, and to see poverty face to face; he could not forget those who were going through with like struggles, and seeing the same dreaded enemy at their doors.

He would not deny himself the privilege of generosity, in order to surround himself with the superfluous elegancies of life.

There was but one luxurious thing in his establishment; that was a couch, soft and easy as modern invention and modern skill could make it. There he loved to see Amy passing her evenings, with her knitting in her hand, while he read aloud, or chatted with the merry-hearted Harriet.

The little family circle was gathered

in the cheerful, comfortable parlor one evening. Will was glancing over the daily paper, when his attention was suddenly arrested by an account of a shipwreck, when cold and wind and sleet were making more treacherous the coast.

"Some of the poor frost-bitten fellows have reached the city, and are at the Marine Hospital. We must do something for them, Amy," said Will, looking up in a glow of kindly sympathy.

"Harriet and I have made up all the flannel Mr. Dimer sent last. I am glad it is ready," said Amy with hearty interest.

"List of the survivors," said Will meditatively, as he ran his eyes along the names. A sudden thrill passed over his frame. Did he see it right? 'Pickard Howe!' There could be but one of that name!

Will checked his sudden exclamation, but his face had told its story to the watchful Amy. Had the hour for which she had been hoping and waiting arrived?

"Pick! Is there news of Pick?" she said, rising as she spoke.

"He was saved! Thank God!" said Will fervently.

The true-hearted brother could not tarry at his comfortable fireside. There was a sufferer at the Marine Hospital, whom he must see ere he slept.

Along the long lines passed William Howe, where every bed was a couch of pain, and every voice was uttering notes of woe. Into each face he gazed anxiously. Would he know his long-lost brother?

Yes—changed, matured, marred was Pickard Howe, yet he could not be mistaken. Those were his light-waving locks, that was his peculiar eye. That face shrinking from the coming stranger, Will knew it at a glance.

"Pick! Brother Pick!" said Will.

The shipwrecked sailor looked up with a start. Years had not changed Will Howe's frank, kindly face. The boy had but become a man, and now the full tenderness of a manly heart was uppermost.

"Oh, Will!" groaned Pick, as he turned away his face.

"Dear Pick! It is such a joy to have you home again," said Will, bending down beside the bed. "Amy will be so glad to see you!"

"Amy—sister Amy! I am not fit to see her!" murmured Pick. "Yet that last prayer of hers brought me home. I could not forget it; and when I lost all by foolishness and sin, and was laid on a bed of sickness, I thought if I could once see her, and hear her say she had forgiven me, I could repent and be a better man."

"She forgave you from the first. She has never ceased to love you and pray for you," said Will tenderly.

"And you, Will, you don't feel hard towards me, or you wouldn't be here," said Pick in a broken voice.

"We are brothers, Pick, and I love you," said Will heartily. "We have a home for you. Your home—your share of the old house. You must come to be happy with us—just where you belong!"

"I don't deserve it! I hope I am a changed man, but—oh, Will! I don't deserve to be welcomed so," said poor Pick!

There was a sound of deep emotion near at hand. The brothers turned quickly; there had been a witness to their meeting.

One who had been long looking after Jesus, and striving in darkness to find him by following his footsteps, was near at hand. The name Pickard Howe had been read by old eyes, who knew that name as belonging to Amy's wandering brother.

"I'll go to him, and do what I can for their sakes!" was Mr. Dimer's first thought; but Will's loving eagerness had forerun the slower steps of the aged man. He had but come in time to hear the words that were blessed to his soul.

"Now, thank God! I believe I am forgiven!" exclaimed the old man. "If Christians can so forgive, I dare trust myself to Jesus—old worn-out sinner that I am!"

CHAPTER XXI.

Conclusion.

THE BROTHERS HOWE was the name of the firm. Brothers they were, in their home and at their business, in their good works and in their prayers. Generosity, tenderness, and forgiveness were met by gratitude, humility, and ever-increasing respectful love.

Sister Amy's heart was full of joy. The troubles of her early life seemed to her as the morning mist, that makes more glorious the coming noonday. She had "borne the yoke in her youth," and the Christian character that was formed, was to her as well-proved armor, that enabled her to go on unharmed and undisturbed through the battles of life.

Amy could rejoice to see Harriet happy and cared for in a home of her

own, without one taint of envy or selfishness. The joy of others was but the
fulfillment of Amy's wishes; and so she
made it her own.

She little knew how Mr. and Mrs.
Alden spoke of her as the "loveliest of
the lovely," and Mr. Dimer called her
"the saint who had beckoned him from
the ways of sin." She felt that she was
in an atmosphere of love, and that her
brothers gave her an affection, deep,
fervent, and true; but she claimed for
herself no share in drawing down her
many blessings on her unworthy head.

Amy's joys were to her the good gifts
of God; and so a bright foreshadowing
of the eternal gladness He loves to
bestow.

The End.

BOOKS BY A.L.O.E.

THE BATTLE (Sequel to *The Giant Killer*)

DASHED TO PIECES

ESCAPE FROM THE EAGLE'S NEST

EXILES IN BABYLON *(Heroes of Faith Series)*

THE GIANT KILLER

THE GOLDEN FLEECE

THE HAUNTED ROOM

HEBREW HEROES

THE JEWEL

NED FRANKS: THE ONE-ARMED SAILOR

THE PASSAGE

PEACE IN WAR

THE PILGRIM'S CALL

PRIDE AND HIS PRISONERS

RESCUED FROM EGYPT *(Heroes of Faith Series)*

THE ROBBERS' CAVE

SHEER OFF!

THE SHEPHERD OF BETHLEHEM *(Heroes of Faith Series)*

TRIUMPH OVER MIDIAN *(Heroes of Faith Series)*

THE WANDERER IN AFRICA

A.L.O.E. (1821-1893) was born Charlotte Maria Tucker near Barnet, Middlesex, England. She was the sixth child of her parents and was educated at home. Under the pseudonym A.L.O.E. (A Lady of England), she wrote over 140 books for children, most with an obvious moral, and devoted the proceeds to charity. In 1875, she left England for India and spent the rest of her life there, engaged in missionary work.

BOOKS BY
CHRISTOPH VON SCHMID

CHRISTOPH VON SCHMID (1768-1854) was born in Bavaria, studied theology, and became an ordained priest in 1791. In 1796 he was placed at the head of a large school, where he began writing stories for children, reading them after school hours as a reward, on condition that the children would write the stories down at home. In 1841, he published a complete edition of his scattered writings in 24 volumes. He is considered the pioneer writer of books for children, and his stories have been translated into at least 24 languages.

1-888-A-GOSPEL • 1-888-246-7735

Books by
Mrs. O.F. Walton

Christie, the King's Servant

Christie's Old Organ

Little Faith

The Lost Clue

My Mates and I

Nobody Loves Me

A Peep Behind the Scenes

Saved at Sea

Throw Me Overboard

When You Least Expect It

Winter's Folly

Mrs. O.F. Walton (1849-1939) was born Amy Catherine Deck in Kent, England. Shortly after her marriage to Octavius Frank Walton, the couple moved to Jerusalem, where Octavius ministered in a church on Mount Zion and Amy wrote *A Peep Behind the Scenes*. Her book *Christie's Old Organ* was one of the earliest books in history of both Christian and children's literature to be translated and published in Japan.

WWW.LAMPLIGHTER.NET

Books by Amy Le Feuvre

Amy Le Feuvre (1861-1929) was born in London, England, and grew up in a large family. She was a prolific author of children's books with a strong Christian message. Her book *Teddy's Button* was one of the most popular of all late Victorian children's stories.

WWW.LAMPLIGHTER.NET

BOOKS OF THE YEAR

Books of the Year are determined by biblical insights, captivating plots, and life-changing character lessons.

- 2020 – QUICKSAND: GETTING TO THE BOTTOM
  – TESTED
- 2019 – PEACE IN WAR
- 2018 – THE TREASURE OF THE SECRET COVE
  – THE SECRET BRIDGE
- 2017 – LAUNCH THE LIFEBOAT
  – ESCAPE FROM THE EAGLE'S NEST
- 2016 – A 'STRORDINARY LITTLE MAID
  – THE LOCKED CUPBOARD
- 2015 – JOSEPH'S SHIELD
  – THE HAUNTED ROOM
- 2014 – FROZEN FIRE
  – COMFORTABLE TROUBLES
- 2013 – IT'S ALL REAL TRUE
  – THE KING'S GOLD
- 2012 – JACK THE CONQUEROR
  – FALSELY ACCUSED
- 2011 – WÄLTY AND THE GREAT GEYER
  – TRUE TO THE LAST
- 2010 – THE WANDERER IN AFRICA
  – THE WHITE GYPSY
- 2009 – SIR MALCOLM AND THE MISSING PRINCE
  – EXILES IN BABYLON
- 2008 – MY MATES AND I
  – THE SHEPHERD OF BETHLEHEM
- 2007 – THE LOST CLUE
- 2006 – ISHMAEL
- 2005 – THE GIANT KILLER
  – THE HIDDEN HAND
- 2004 – THE CROSS TRIUMPHANT
- 2003 – SIR KNIGHT OF THE SPLENDID WAY
- 2002 – SHIPWRECKED, BUT NOT LOST
- 2001 – TEDDY'S BUTTON
- 2000 – THE HEDGE OF THORNS
- 1999 – THE LAMPLIGHTER
- 1998 – A PEEP BEHIND THE SCENES
- 1997 – TITUS: A COMRADE OF THE CROSS
- 1996 – THE BASKET OF FLOWERS

1-888-A-GOSPEL • 1-888-246-7735

Illustrated books

We are delighted to present to you this creative collection with beautiful illustrations for young visual learners. Reinforce character building and stimulate imagination with our Illustrated Collection. To view the complete collection, visit www.lamplighter.net.

Trusty: Tried and True
Written by Mark Hamby, *Really* written by Debbie Hamby
Illustrated by Jennifer Brandon

This adorable adventure is bursting with colorful imagery to heighten a child's imagination and stir creativity. Learn about selfishness, pride, and vanity through the characters of Brawny, Smarty, and Beauty, and be inspired by our hero Trusty, who courageously tries to help. This will surely become a family favorite to be read over and over again!

Teddy's Button, Illustrated
Rewritten by Mark Hamby

Join Teddy in his mischievous adventures as he discovers that you don't win the battle with guns and hate, you win the battle with love, and your greatest enemy is yourself. You will never forget what happens when Teddy enlists in the Lord's army!

The Three Weavers, Illustrated
Rewritten by Mark Hamby
Illustrated by Jennifer Brandon

A delightful allegory for fathers to read with their daughters—not just once, but over and over again. This illustrated rendition reveals how each weaver prepares his daughter to weave a mantle perfectly suited for the prince. But each father uses a different approach, and the consequences are very revealing! Enjoy many thought-provoking conversations, creating memories for years to come.

LAMPLIGHTER THEATRE

Lamplighter Theatre helps to fulfill the mission of Lamplighter by bringing redemptive hope to the world through dramatic audio. Forged through the commitment and sacrifice of a dedicated team, Lamplighter Theatre now airs on 1800 radio stations in 29 countries. With the talent of world-renowned actors, writers, directors, music composers, and sound engineers, Lamplighter Theatre creatively brings redemptive hope to broken lives, and compels its listeners to live life skillfully and sacrificially for the benefit of others.

SIR MALCOLM AND THE MISSING PRINCE
2-DISC AUDIO DRAMA

Inside the castle walls a battle rages in the heart of a widowed king. His son, the young Prince Hubert, has proven himself to be an unworthy heir to the throne. But a bold intervention by the king's most trusted knight could prove to be the cure. In the remote lands of this vast kingdom, far from the walls of the palace, Hugh will learn that the requirement of kingship is servanthood. *Best for ages 6-11.*

Approximate Time: 2 hrs.

FROZEN FIRE
2-DISC AUDIO DRAMA

The events that lead up to Betty's pivotal decision demonstrate the true meaning of humility, servanthood, and love. Inspired by a true story, Betty must come face to face with a dreaded foe. Facing myriad trials, including abandonment and the death-

grip of a terrifying blizzard, her love for her devoted servant trumps all. You will fall in love with Betty, whose loyalty is demonstrated through tremendous courage and sacrifice. *Frozen Fire* will keep you on the edge of your seat! Great for the entire family.

Approximate Time: 2 hrs.

Learn more, listen to samples, and view entire drama collection at
WWW.LAMPLIGHTER.NET

BEST FOR...

The 'Best For' Collections are designed for those individuals who have seen this engaging collection of books and wondered which would be best for their children. We have selected an array of stories for each age group to give you just a taste of what Lamplighter books are all about.

BEST FOR AGES 6-11

Basil; Or, Honesty and Industry

Christie's Old Organ

The Giant Killer

Helen's Temper

Jack the Conqueror

Jessica's First Prayer

Jill's Red Bag

Joseph's Shield

Little Sir Galahad

Little Threads

Probable Sons

Teddy's Button

The White Dove

BEST FOR AGES 9-14

The Basket of Flowers

The Captive

The Golden Thread

The Hedge of Thorns

The Little Lamb

My Golden Ship

Hand on the Bridle

A Peep Behind the Scenes

Rising to the Top

The Robbers' Cave

Rosa of Linden Castle

Shipwrecked, But Not Lost

The White Knights

BEST FOR AGES 12-99

The Alabaster Box

Escape from the Eagle's Nest

The Haunted Room

The Hidden Hand

Ishmael

The Lamplighter

The Lost Clue

Sir Knight of the Splendid Way

The White Gypsy

WWW.LAMPLIGHTER.NET

*my*LAMPLIGHTER
BOOK & AUDIO CLUB

The *myLamplighter Book Club* allows you to follow your own personalized strategic plan as you make a wise investment for your family. We are offering you the opportunity to own the entire Lamplighter collection at your own pace, so that you are in control of your investment.

- · SIMPLICITY – YOU choose which titles you would like to receive each month.
- · SAVINGS – YOU decide how much money you'd like to save each month!
- · CONVENIENCE – YOU maintain and update your account anytime, anywhere.

You can switch plans or temporarily put your club on hold.
You can remove titles from your queue.
You can update and maintain your account online.
Shipping is FREE! *Book Club is not offered outside the US.*
Membership is FREE!
Character Comprehension Quizzes are FREE - $199 value!

PLAN 1	**1 Book per month**
PLAN 2	**2 Books per month**
PLAN 3	**3 Books per month**
PLAN 4	**4 Books per month**

Book Club members can add a New Release at any time to any plan at a 15% discount and free shipping.

TO SIGN UP
Log in at www.lamplighter.net/book-audio-club.

1-888-A-GOSPEL • 1-888-246-7735

THE
LAMPLIGHTER MISSION

Printing books of high quality with an emphasis on character development, biblical insights, artistic design, excellence, and skilled craftsmanship is an integral part of the Lamplighter Mission. Guided by our mission "to make ready a people prepared for the Lord" (Luke 1:17), Lamplighter Publishing and Bindery is strategically engaged by building Christlike character one story at a time. Through the mystery and adventure of Lamplighter stories, the framework of character development is formed and the pursuit of excellence is cultivated. The dominant theme of hope is developed by characters who persevere in adversity, being fully convinced that nothing is impossible with God.

It is the Lamplighter commitment that each book instills moral values through role models that either demonstrate exemplary behavior or suffer the consequences of making wrong choices. A riveting plot, a worthy theme, and endearing characters will motivate readers, both young and old, to adopt a similar moral code by emulating the characters that have now been etched into their awakened conscience.

The goal of Lamplighter Ministries is to cultivate a renaissance of creative excellence that inspires one to know God intimately and proclaim Him passionately. At the Lamplighter Guild, students have the opportunity to work alongside world-class actors, scriptwriters, sound designers, music composers, oil painters, theologians, culinary artists, and other master teachers.

Through these masters, Lamplighter Theatre was established, providing a platform from which Lamplighter books are adapted into classic audio dramas now aired in over 30 countries. Lamplighter Ministries stands on the shoulders of those who have built a good foundation. It is our commitment to remain faithful to these high standards and inspire others to do the same and more. In the words of Solomon, "Do you see a man skillful in his work? He will stand before kings; he will not stand before obscure men" (Proverbs 22:29).

For more information about Lamplighter Ministries, visit www.lamplighter.net or www.lamplighterguild.com. To order a free catalog go to www.lamplighter.net or call toll free 1-888-A-GOSPEL (1-888-246-7735).

LAMPLIGHTER *Publishing*

BUILDING CHRISTLIKE CHARACTER ... ONE STORY AT A TIME

ALSO AVAILABLE FROM LAMPLIGHTER:

CHARACTER COMPREHENSION QUIZZES:
Help children interact with the content from Lamplighter Books with Lamplighter's Character Comprehension Quizzes and interactive iQuizzes. Now available online at *www.lamplighter.net*.

To request a catalog, please contact us:
Phone: *1-888-246-7735* or
1-570-585-1314
Email: *mail@lamplighter.net*
or visit our website at *www.lamplighter.net*.

ISBN 978-1-58474-045-2

51800 >

9 781584 740452